TRUTH OR DARE

TRUTH OR DARE

Barbara Dee

ALADDIN

New York London Toronto Sydney New Delhi

ALADDIN

An imprint of Simon & Schuster Children's Publishing Division

1230 Avenue of the Americas, New York, New York 10020

First Aladdin hardcover edition September 2016

Text copyright © 2016 by Barbara Dee

Jacket illustration copyright © 2016 by Jeanine Henderson

All rights reserved, including the right of reproduction in whole or in part in any form.

ALADDIN is a trademark of Simon & Schuster, Inc., and related logo is a registered trademark of Simon & Schuster, Inc.

For information about special discounts for bulk purchases, please contact Simon & Schuster Special Sales at 1-866-506-1949 or business@simonandschuster.com.

The Simon & Schuster Speakers Bureau can bring authors to your live event. For more information or to book an event contact the Simon & Schuster Speakers Bureau at 1-866-248-3049 or visit our website at www.simonspeakers.com.

Book designed by Laura Lyn DiSiena

The text of this book was set in Minion.

Manufactured in the United States of America 0816 FFG

10 9 8 7 6 5 4 3 2 1

This book has been cataloged with the Library of Congress.

ISBN 978-1-4814-5968-6 (hc)

ISBN 978-1-4814-5970-9 (eBook)

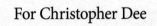
For Christopher Dee

TRUTH OR DARE

The Comma Club

I RIPPED OPEN THE BOX, AND THERE I WAS.

My name, times five hundred.

Amalia Jessica Rollins.

Seeing my name in print always gave me a weird feeling. But this wasn't just weird. It was wrong.

Not even asking me for input, Dad had ordered five hundred labels for the stuff I was bringing to sleepaway camp. How had he come up with the number five hundred? Even if I labeled every bristle on my toothbrush, I didn't own half that many things altogether.

And the font. It was all frilly and girly, like what you'd use to invite someone to a tea party. *This is my sock. Sorry it smells like feet. I say, would you care for a crumpet?*

Plus, he'd ordered the wrong name. *Nobody* called me Amalia, which sounded like a fussy old lady who wore lace collars, or maybe an old-timey girl who played piano for her cat. I was just Lia, definitely not a lace-collar sort of person, and I couldn't play piano, except for "Chopsticks."

And if I stuck all these labels on my clothes and towels and stuff, I'd be spending the entire summer going, *Actually, it's Lia. No, just Lia. L-I-A. You pronounce it Lee-uhh.*

Another thing: He'd included my middle name. Using your middle name on camp labels made you sound kind of like a baby. The fact that Jessica was also my mom's name—well, I didn't need five hundred labels to remind me about her. It's not like I'd forgotten anything in two and a half years.

And if all that wasn't enough, the labels Dad had ordered were *iron-on*. Abi's mom had told him to get the stick-on kind, but maybe he forgot. Or else he remembered that Mom had always used the iron-on kind, so he assumed they worked better. Maybe they did—but I was supposed to leave for camp in two days. I didn't know the first thing about how to iron. Even if I downloaded some instructions, ironing labels—*five hundred!*—at the end of a scorching June sounded to me like medieval torture.

I plopped onto my bed.

All my camp clothes—shorts, tees, swimsuits, jeans, socks, pj's, sweaters, raincoat, underwear—were piled in semi-neat stacks on my bedroom floor, waiting for somebody to pack them. Me, obviously. Well, I could just write *Lia Rollins* on everything in Sharpie, couldn't I? But what if the ink ran in the rain, or in the washing machine, and all the clothing I owned got smeared? Or what if the ink bled through to the other side, and so my back said *snilloR aiL*?

That would be horrific. *Actually, no, it's Lia. Read it backward, okay? Just pretend I'm standing in a mirror!*

Then it occurred to me: I could ask Abi's mom to help me iron. Abi's mom was like the Mom in Chief of Maplebrook. Plus, she was the leader of what Dad calls the Mom Squad, all my friends' moms who pitched in after Mom's accident. Abi's mom—she made us call her Val—was constantly saying, *You can call me anytime, Lia. About anything.*

So maybe I could call her now and say, *Hi there, Val. How would you feel about ironing labels? Even though Dad ignored your advice about the stick-ons?*

Okay, maybe not.

I reached under my bed, which was where I stored all my collections in bins: buttons, seashells, erasers, marbles, charms, dice. I opened the bin of marbles and started sorting them by color, which usually relaxed me.

"Lia?" My fourteen-year-old brother, Nate, was in the doorway. "Friend for you downstairs."

"Now? Who?" I sat up.

"I dunno. All your little friends look the same to me. Except for Jules."

"Shut up," I said. I was sick of his comments about Jules. "Is it Abi? Makayla? Marley?"

I'd tossed my cell phone exactly two and a half years ago, vowing never to get a new one. This meant friends of mine were always showing up without the "can-I-come-over-now" call first. It wasn't a problem for me, but it got on my brother's nerves.

He shrugged. "Go see for yourself, Lia, okay? She's in the kitchen."

I ran downstairs. Marley was standing at the counter. She was wearing a baggy Maplebrook Middle School tee and jeans with holes in the knees, and she was holding a Tupperware.

"Hey," I said.

She grinned. Marley's orthodontist let her change the colors of her rubber bands every visit, and now, for some reason, they were purple and orange. Her mouth always looked as if she were rooting for a team I'd never heard of.

"I came to say good-bye," she announced. "For the summer. Also, my mom made you these. She wants the container back, so . . ." She handed me a Tupperware. I took off the lid: oatmeal cookies.

"Yum," I said. "Tell her thanks."

"They have raisins," Marley said. "Sorry."

"What's wrong with raisins?" I took a big bite of cookie.

"They're all shriveled up." She made a face like a raisin. "I like food that's smooth."

Marley could be a little weird sometimes, but she was smart. Sometimes people thought she was sort of slow, because she had "a learning thing," which meant that she had a bunch of different aides and tutors at school and also at home. But I knew how fast her brain worked and how she noticed things. Also how incredible she was at drawing.

Plus, there was another thing about her: She was the only friend I had who looked like me.

I don't mean in the face. (I was green-eyed and light-brown-haired, with a turned-up nose and pale freckles on my cheeks. Marley had dark brown eyes and dark brown hair and messy bangs and wore black glasses that practically shouted *nerd*. But on her they looked cool; I can't explain why, but they did.)

I mean in the body. Of all our friends, Marley and

I were the Least Developed. Neither of us had boobs or waists or hips, and we were both skinny as spaghetti. Julianna—who everyone called Jules—was Most Developed; she'd had her period since the start of sixth grade and made sure we knew about it every month. ("Omigod, I have killer cramps," she always said, which sounded to me like a cheesy sci-fi movie: *Attack of the Killer Cramps. Return of the Killer Cramps.*) Makayla and Abi—which was short for Abigail—were both "on the verge," they said, constantly talking about and comparing "symptoms."

But Marley and I weren't even close to being "on the verge." We were both in the Comma Club, we joked—comma as opposed to period, haha. (This was a private joke, by the way; we didn't share it with our other friends. At least, I didn't.)

Marley was spending this summer with her dad in Chicago, going to art school at some museum. And suddenly it occurred to me how much I was going to miss her.

"I wish you were doing camp with us," I blurted.

"Not me." She shuddered. "I hate spiders. And sitting around the campfire, toasting things."

"We don't toast *things*. We toast *marshmallows*. And it's not like that's all we do for ten weeks."

"Yeah, okay. But the whole cabin business." She caught my eye.

"What about it?" I asked.

"I don't know. Living with the same people all the time. Eating with them, listening to them snore, changing clothes in front of them . . ."

I didn't need to ask; I could guess what she meant. Marley still wore undershirts. I had a couple of "training bras" Val gave me after Abi must have asked her to. Training bra: The idea was funny, if you thought about it. Like you needed to train yourself to wear underwear. *Oh, good job; you're really wearing that thing correctly today!*

"But it won't be *so* bad," Marley added quickly. "I mean, you have Jules and Abi and Makayla—"

"Yeah. But there are twelve girls in our cabin, not just them. I wish—"

"What?"

"Nothing. No, you're right. We'll have an awesome summer. So will you."

Marley threw her arms around me and squeezed. "I'd say I'll write to you, but you know I won't. See you in September, Lia."

"See you, Marley. Bye. No, wait!"

Except she ran out the front door before I could give her back the plastic container.

The You-Know-What

TWO DAYS LATER I WAS MEETING THE CAMP Sunflower Hill bus in the shopping center parking lot. Dad, who was an optometrist, had taken off work that morning so he could bring me over, even though Val had insisted she could do it. But at the last minute some patient needed emergency sunglasses or something, so he was on the phone when we should have been driving. And by the time we got to the shopping center, my friends were already waiting in the parking lot, with their duffel bags and backpacks piled beside them.

"Lia!" Abi screamed as I joined them. "We thought you'd forgotten! Where are all your bags?"

"In the car." I pointed to where Dad was standing, nodding slowly while Val was giving a speech to him about sunscreen.

"Well, aren't you *bringing* them?" Abi laughed. She always laughed at the end of sentences, even if what she said wasn't funny.

"Yeah, I will," I said. "In a minute."

"But the bus will be here in, like, thirty seconds. You should go get them; I'll help you carry them."

"It's okay. I'll get them myself. But thanks, Abi."

She made a "whatever" face.

Then Jules threw her arms around me in a squeezy hug. Last year Jules was just sort of blobby; this year when she hugged me, it always gave me a little shock. I mean, it felt almost like hugging a grown-up. Today she was wearing a sundress a few shades yellower than her hair, and you could see purple bra straps peeking out from both shoulders. All of Jules's clothes were hand-me-downs from her fashion-obsessed big sister, so everything Jules wore was the latest style, although from three years ago. Not that any of us was counting.

"So did Abi tell you?" Jules murmured.

"Tell me what?" I glanced at Abi, who usually was in charge of information.

"About Makayla. She got her you-know-what."

"Her period?"

"Last night. Finally."

"It was really, really baaaad," Abi said, doing an exaggerated wince. I looked at Makayla, who was standing a few feet away with her mom. Of all of us, Makayla was the best student, the best athlete, and (in my opinion) the best-looking. She was tall and strong, half African-American (her dad) and half Korean (her mom); her skin was warm brown, and her long black hair made a thick, wavy ponytail. She was captain of the district swim team, played flute in the countywide band, and wasn't afraid to stand up to anybody, even Abi. I was in awe of Makayla, to be honest, but right then she looked droopy and weepy.

She must have noticed that I was staring, because she said something to her mom and walked over.

"Hey, Lia." She gave a crooked smile. "So you heard the big news?"

I nodded. "You okay?"

"Sure. If it's okay to feel like your body's been taken over by aliens."

Jules smiled sympathetically. "Is that how it feels to

you? Because whenever I get killer cramps, I think of them like mice playing on gym equipment."

"That's horrible," Abi said, laughing.

"To me the cramps feel bigger and slower," Makayla said thoughtfully. "Like maybe a giant sea monster walking through peanut butter."

"That's pretty good," Jules said. "My sister says it feels like they're taking down a building. With one of those wrecking-ball things."

I started to chew on my cuticles.

"Plus I have a headache," Makayla added.

Jules nodded. "A throbbing one?"

"No. More like my head is a gum-ball machine."

"Well, that's better than a pinball machine!" Jules said. "That's what *my* headaches always feel like!"

"And I just feel so *bleh,*" Makayla said. "And slow. Like a slimy slug."

"Well, at least you don't *look* too bad," Abi said.

"Are you serious, Abi?" Makayla groaned. "My stomach is completely bloated. My hair's a mess. My skin is supergross—"

I took a couple of steps backward.

"Lia, where are you going?" Abi asked.

"Bags," I said as I turned and started jogging. "Back in a sec."

I stopped in front of Dad, who was telling Val something about his Check Engine light. "Excuse me? Dad?" I said, out of breath. "Can I please talk to you a minute? Inside the car?"

"Everything okay, Lia?" Val asked, her made-up eyes concerned and piercing.

I nodded. "Great."

Dad and I got in the car. "What's up, Doc?" he asked, patting my knee.

I took a deep breath. "I'm not going."

"You mean to camp?"

"Yeah. Sorry. It was a huge mistake."

He smiled patiently. "Oh, come on, Lee-lee. It's normal to feel a little nervous—"

"I'm not nervous. I just don't want to *do* it."

He stopped smiling. "What happened?"

"Nothing."

"Then what's changed? Lia, you've been to sleepaway camp before. You loved it. A week ago you were so excited to go back."

"I don't want to talk about it, okay?"

His eyebrows rose. "You're not even going to give me a reason?"

"I can't. It's too personal."

"Well, you need to tell me *something*."

"Okay." I stared out the window at my friends. Abi, Makayla, and Jules had their arms around one another's shoulders, and they were singing, but I couldn't tell what. Val was chatting with Makayla's mother, and Jules's mom was smearing sunscreen on her elbows.

"I didn't iron on the labels," I said.

"What?"

"The labels you ordered. They were all wrong. The font was horrific, and it wasn't even my right *name*, so I can't possibly go to camp, or all my stuff will get lost."

"Oh." He blinked. In this light, I could see his eyes behind his sunglasses. They looked tired. "Well, Lee-lee, I'm sure someone at camp can help you label your clothing—"

"But that's not everything," I blurted. "Please don't make me talk about it, okay? I just don't want to go. I've changed my mind. Please, Daddy?"

He sighed. I never called him Daddy anymore, and it probably startled him a little to hear it. Also, I never asked him for anything. Ever since Mom's accident, I made myself be as easy as possible. Sometimes Nate was moody and gave Dad backtalk, but not me. I just wanted there to be no more problems.

So maybe that was why he seemed to be thinking it over. "Well, aside from the fact that I already paid for the summer and don't even know how much I can get back, there's the issue of *you*. I've got to go to work, obviously. And Nate has travel baseball—"

"I know. I wouldn't hang out with him, anyway."

"And all your friends will be gone. So how will you entertain yourself all summer?"

"I'll stay with Aunt Shelby." As soon as I said this, I knew it was a brilliant plan. Aunt Shelby had a beach house up in Maine, and she'd been begging me to visit for "girl time." Dad always said Aunt Shelby was "a nut," and Nate always said she was just plain crazy. It wasn't that I disagreed with them, to be honest. But Aunt Shelby was also Mom's younger sister, the only grown-up female relative I had.

Dad scratched his chin for a few seconds. Then he said, "Has she invited you?"

"Only like a million times."

"I'll have to think—" he said slowly.

I kissed his cheek fast, so he couldn't.

And right at that moment I could see the camp bus pulling into the parking lot. It was shiny and silver, bigger than a school bus, and it probably had a bathroom. Probably played videos too.

"Dad? Can we please just leave now?" I begged.

He grunted. "I don't know about this, Lia. You don't even want to tell your friends you're not coming with them?"

"Truthfully? No."

"Well." We sat there and watched the bus come up to the curb. Abi was looking at our car, waving her arm like, *Hurry up, Lia! What's taking you so long?* And Val began jogging toward us with a concerned-mom look on her face. I couldn't watch.

"Your mom would never agree to this, you know," Dad murmured.

"I know."

"As long as you do," he said, and we zoomed off.

Mom Squad

I GUESS IT'S TIME TO TELL YOU WHAT HAPPENED
with Mom. I've put it off as long as I could, but nothing
will make sense if I don't explain it. So here goes. Two
and a half years ago Mom was driving home from work.
She taught first grade at Maplebrook Elementary and
had to stay late that day for some faculty meeting. It was
dark and raining when the meeting ended, so she took
the long way home, because the streetlights were better.
But some stupid guy in a stupid SUV was talking on
his stupid cell phone, and instead of paying attention

to a stop sign, he slammed his car into Mom's. And he killed her.

At first I was just kind of in shock. All I kept thinking was, I wonder what that guy was talking about on his stupid cell phone. Like, what could possibly have been so important that it was *more* important than being careful about my mom? *Hey, did you see the game last night?* or *Honey, I'm sorry I'm running late, but there was traffic.* Or, *Did you see that skating cat on YouTube? Dude, it was hilarious.*

After the funeral the guy actually came to our house to apologize. He was bald and pudgy, crying into a handkerchief, and he came with his wife, who brought us cookies. The fancy bakery kind that look all fake, pink and green with rainbow sprinkles that taste like wax. Dad let them sit on our sofa and apologize for a few minutes, while Nate and I watched from upstairs. Dad didn't say very much, and then he stood, which meant it was time for them to leave. But the guy started blubbering, so finally Dad left them alone in the living room.

"That poor man," was all he said to us afterward.

But Nate and I didn't think he was a poor man. We thought he was a monster. Not the fairy-tale kind, but the real kind, who were actually scarier, because they acted "sorry."

So we tossed the cookies in the trash. And while we

were at it, I also tossed my cell phone. It didn't make a whole lot of sense, I knew—I mean, *I* wasn't the person who'd been blabbing instead of paying attention to driving a car. But just the thought of using it again made me sick. And even though Nate told me I was being crazy, that it was like I was punishing myself when it wasn't my fault, I didn't care. No more cell phone for me again. Ever.

My friends didn't question my decision, even though it made it hard for them to communicate with me. So they visited my house a lot after the funeral, hanging out in my bedroom or watching dumb movies with me on the downstairs TV.

The only one who didn't come over all the time was Marley. But for the whole rest of that year, she made me a drawing every day. The drawings weren't about my mom or what happened to her—they were pretty random, actually: a tiger hiding in tall grass, a flying dragon, baby penguins. Marley never said anything about these draw-ings; she just slipped them into my mailbox or put them on my desk at school. But I knew what they meant, that she was thinking of me, and for a long time they were what I looked forward to.

In the days after the Accident (that's what we called it, "the Accident," even though the guy wasn't on his cell "by accident"), people kept coming over to our house with food—casseroles, lasagnas, layer cakes, salads, roast chickens, meat loaves, stews, pies. They must have thought losing Mom made us hungry. The truth was, none of us had any appetite, so Dad ended up donating a lot of the meals to a local food pantry. And even though that made us feel a bit better, we still felt guilty about finding so much food on our doorstep every day. Guilty, and also (weirdly) ashamed, like people thought we couldn't take care of ourselves anymore.

Finally, after a couple of weeks, Val showed up in our kitchen with her mom-ponytail and a lime green yoga jacket, even though she didn't do yoga. She was carrying a huge blue mug of coffee and a pink spiral notebook. "All right, Rollins family, here's the thing," she said in her take-charge voice. "People want to help. I know you don't want all this food right now, but you'll need meals down the road. Oh." She cleared her throat, as if she'd realized she shouldn't use the expression "down the road."

"Val, that's very thoughtful of you, but—" Dad began.

"Kevin, I know what you're going to say: You can cook for yourselves. Please." She held up a hand, her nails polished a dark pink. "You'll probably just order pizza every night. That's not going to cut it; you guys need to stay strong. And you need to let people feel better by doing something."

She flipped open her notebook. I could see that she'd drawn a calendar in different colors of ink.

"We're delivering meals to you on Tuesdays and Fridays," she announced. "For the foreseeable future. We have loads of people who want to cook, so if we rotate volunteers, it won't be a burden to anyone. But what else can we do? Shopping? Driving? You name it."

"Val," Dad said, shaking his head.

"Not a choice, Kevin. We're helping, and you can't stop us." She laughed the way Abi did—loud and a little hoarse, like a punctuation mark at the end of her sentence.

And that's how the Mom Squad started. After a few months the neighbors and Mom's friends gradually stopped delivering meals, but not Val. She kept bringing over huge feasts every Tuesday: baked ziti, stuffed peppers, minestrone, garlic bread, tossed salads with slivered almonds, chocolate chip cookies so fresh out of the oven that the chocolate was still melty.

"She cooks like this every night?" Nate said one time. "No wonder Abi's fat."

"Shut up," I told him. "Abi isn't *fat*. And don't talk like that. You should be grateful—"

"Dude, I totally *am* grateful," he replied. I could tell by the way he blushed that he meant it, too.

My other friends' moms couldn't cook like Val, so she

organized them in different ways. Makayla's mom worked long hours, so she had a cleaning service once a week; after the Accident, she sent the cleaners over to our house sometimes. Jules's mom helped out with our shopping. Marley's mom planted daffodil bulbs in our front yard and brought us vegetables from her garden. The Mom Squad ran other errands, too, while Dad was at work all day, and constantly invited us over for meals. But everything was still organized through Val, who kept up her calendar in different-colored markers.

And during this time Aunt Shelby drove down from Maine every few weeks or so for visits. She was Mom's only sibling, her younger sister—but she and Dad were such opposites that it didn't make sense for her to stay longer than a weekend. For one thing, she always talked about how she'd hated growing up in Maplebrook, how "boring" and "stifling" it was here, how all the people in town (for example, Val) "gave her seizures." She'd even ask Dad how he could "stand" being an optometrist.

"What's wrong with my job?" he'd reply, winking at me.

"Nothing. Except isn't what you do all day holding up lenses to people's eyes? And asking them, over and over, 'Better? Or worse?'"

"That's how we fit lenses," he'd say patiently.

"Yes, but to spend your precious time on this planet dividing experience into 'better or worse,'" she'd answer. "I mean, really, Kevin. Don't you want to scream sometimes?"

Nate and I would just look at each other and shrug. We didn't have any idea what she was going on about. Had she picked on Dad like this in front of Mom? I couldn't remember. But I did remember Mom and Aunt Shelby constantly arguing—usually behind closed doors, so the rest of us couldn't listen. And sometimes their arguments got so bad they didn't speak to each other for weeks.

Since the Accident, though, Aunt Shelby was around all the time; at least, it felt that way. As soon as she would arrive in her rusty old pickup truck, wearing big billowy dresses covered with cat fur, Val would clear out. We wouldn't see Val, or the rest of the Mom Squad, for the entire weekend. And right away the kitchen would turn into a crazy, messy Shelby-lab, with pots boiling sour-smelling leaves and the blender mixing juices from vegetables I'd never heard of.

"You should try some of this soup, Kevin," Aunt Shelby would urge him. "It'll help your stress level. The ancient Inca—"

"My stress level doesn't need help from the ancient Inca," he'd mutter.

"But it's therapeutic. You think Western doctors are the only ones who know how to treat stress?"

"No, Shelby," Dad would say, smiling stiffly. "I don't.

And if I'm stressed, maybe it's because you keep forcing me to eat things."

She never tried to get Nate and me to take any of that stuff, which was a good thing. We'd become so spoiled with Val's cooking that if something didn't taste chocolaty or cheesy, we weren't interested.

And the truth was, we were doing okay without our aunt's smelly soups. By "okay," I'm not saying we weren't sad about Mom, because we were. I mean, we were *incredibly* sad. But Nate had his baseball team, and I had my friends, plus the constant hugs and attention of the Mom Squad. And whenever I felt jittery or lonesome at home, I'd pick up a book, or I'd sort through my collections. And time would pass—sometimes too much time—while I organized tiny things by color or size.

But especially at night, in the minutes before I drifted off to sleep, I'd feel a kind of dull ache in my chest, a missing-Mom ache. When I got that ache, I couldn't distract myself with marbles or books. Or with anything else, for that matter. And more and more, especially lately, there were things I wished I could discuss with her—not with Dad, or Val, or anybody else.

For example, friend stuff. Did Mom have a group of best friends when she was in seventh grade? What were they like? Did they all go off together to sleepaway camp, or split up for the summer, like we just did? Did she feel behind them in big, important ways—like developing boobs and getting her period? How did she survive any of it—the way girls checked one another out and competed about "symptoms," the way boys commented on who was "fat" and who was pretty?

Also: Did she have a crush? Was he like mine—a secret from her friends? And if she did have a crush, did he ever find out about it? Did anything happen with him? Could she give me any details? (But only if hearing the details wouldn't be too weird.)

Every time Aunt Shelby visited, she said we needed "special time" for "girl talk." But I'd never wanted this "special time," not with her. She was so strange and even a little bit witchy, I thought, with her loose dresses, her long, skinny braids, and her funny-smelling potions. Plus, she didn't care what she said, even if it hurt people's feelings.

But now, for some crazy reason, the thought of "special time" with her seemed like something I could handle. And anyway, I told myself, staying with Aunt Shelby let me hide out from camp.

Up in Maine, away from Maplebrook.

Away from everything. Everybody.

Including—no, especially—my best friends.

Girls Just Wanna Have Fun

DAD DROVE ME UP TO AUNT SHELBY'S THAT weekend. It was an especially hot day, even for that boiling June, and by the time we arrived in Benchley, Maine, we were both sweaty and limp. Aunt Shelby's beach house had a small, rickety porch, where she was sitting in a rocking chair with a cat on her lap. As soon as we drove up the sandy driveway, she let out a shriek and the cat went flying.

"Lia! My little niecelet!" She threw her arms around me. "I wasn't sure you'd actually materialize!"

"But I did," I said, inhaling my aunt's personal smell,

kind of a cross between dried lavender and sardines. For an entire minute she wouldn't stop hugging me. Some hair that got loose from one of her braids got into my mouth, and I didn't want to be rude by spitting it out. But finally I brushed it away with my free hand.

"Oh, we're going to have so much fun!" she squealed. All of a sudden she was making me dance a ridiculous tango. "Girls just wanna have fu-unn," she sang.

I giggled, even though we probably looked slightly insane. Over her shoulder I could see Dad, who was either squinting in the sunshine or trying not to wince.

"Oh, wait!" Aunt Shelby suddenly cried. She pulled away from me. "Where are my manners? I made some banana bread. And there's iced tea!"

"None for me, thanks," Dad said.

"Aw, c'mon," she said in a teasing voice. "It's just plain old boring Snapple. I didn't sneak anything else in there, I promise."

"I'm sure you didn't. And I appreciate it, Shelby. But it's getting late, and I promised Nate I'd be home before dark, so . . ."

"Understood. No worries, Kevin."

Something passed between them, and I had the feeling once again that Dad didn't *like* her. Well, it wouldn't be too surprising, I decided, the way she was always criticizing his job and where he lived. And with her soups and everything, she was definitely pushy—but she was Mom's little sister, after all. And you had to admit she was really nice to let me stay with her all summer. Especially considering that we'd asked her about it only two days before I got there.

Dad opened the trunk and took out my two duffel bags still marked LIA ROLLINS, CAMP SUNFLOWER HILL in black Sharpie. They looked awkward sitting there on the porch, basically announcing that camp had been a mistake. A gray cat—not the same one who'd jumped off Aunt Shelby's lap—tiptoed over and began to sniff them.

"Well, kiddo," Dad said, putting his hands on my shoulders. "Be a good houseguest. Help your aunt with chores. And don't run with the wolves."

"Wait. What?" I said.

"He's joking," Aunt Shelby said, grinning. "There are no wolves on the beach. Unless you count teen boys."

Dad acted as if he didn't hear her. Instead he looked straight into my eyes. "I expect to hear from you once in a while, Lee-lee."

"Oh, you will," Aunt Shelby said brightly. "Cell service is spotty up here, but she can borrow my phone anytime."

He looked at her and nodded. Then he smiled at me. "Have fun," he said quietly. "That's your job this summer, okay?"

"Dad?" I swallowed. "Thanks."

"Thank your aunt, not me."

He kissed my forehead, got into the car, waved once, and drove off.

Aunt Shelby's cottage was a mess, but in a good way, kind of how a kid's room would be if no one made her clean. Her living room was tiny, just a wicker love seat and an overstuffed chair that had been shredded by cats, a small kidney-shaped table piled high with books, and a few dusty plants. On the ceiling were strung-up kites—a butterfly, a dragon, a pterodactyl, a red-tailed hawk. Her kitchen was a smaller version of the crazy lab she always made at our house, with a zillion glass jars on the windowsill and two pots simmering on the stove. An expandable wooden table was pushed to the wall, along with three chairs painted red, one of which had a seat that was held together with silver duct tape. In the middle of the table was a mason jar filled with grapefruit-size peonies that shed pink petals on the checkerboard linoleum.

On the other side of the living room were two narrow bedrooms, hers (iron bed with gauzy quilts and a zillion faded pillows, dresses tossed on the window seat and on the floor) and mine (futon to sleep on, three wobbly bookshelves stuffed with books and boxes, an exercise bike that she used for a scarf rack). Even though all the windows were open, the air smelled like old soup; and even though the floors were bare, when you walked shoeless, your toes were tickled by sand and cat fur.

It wasn't perfect. But it was a zillion times better than being at camp.

"Lia, you need to meet my babies," Aunt Shelby declared. "Only problem is getting them to introduce themselves." Somehow she managed to scoop up six cats: Pashmina, Stinkbug, Escobar, Brunhilda, Archie, and Doomhammer.

"They're all so cute," I said, stroking the smallest one, Doomhammer. "I've always wanted a cat, but Mom was allergic."

"Jessie? No, she wasn't." Aunt Shelby snorted. "That's what she *said*. She just didn't *like* them." She picked up the one named Escobar and nuzzled his orange-striped head. "How could anyone not like *you*?" she crooned.

I wondered if that was true—that my mom had made up a story about cat allergies. But why would Aunt Shelby lie about that? "Why do you have so many?" I asked, to change the subject.

"You think this is a lot? I used to have more, actually. My friends at Benchley Rescues keep giving me these beauties to foster, and I end up keeping them. I guess I'm too nurturing for my own good."

She dropped Escobar, as if she'd just remembered something. "Oh, and also there's Demon Spawn. She's mostly outdoors, so she isn't officially a family member. But she stops by every few days for some kibble. What are your plans, exactly?"

"Me?"

"For the summer."

"Oh." I hadn't thought about *plans*. "Well, I was hoping to spend time on the beach. I'd like to get some more shells, and I wanted to start collecting sea glass. And I'm reading this book—"

"Oh yeah? Anything good?"

Before I'd left, Dad had given me the complete Hiber-Nation trilogy about this future society where girls go underground until they're grown-ups. I started to explain the plot of Book One, which is all about this girl named Bree who pretends to be asleep while secretly organizing a girl revolt. It was the best book ever, even if it didn't get made into a movie.

Before I could finish describing the plot, Aunt Shelby

cut me off. "Wow, that sounds really exciting. But I was wondering if you'd mind hanging out a bit in the shop. Just mornings."

"The shop?"

"Herb 'n' Renewal. I sell homeopathic treatments—herbs, teas, you name it. You knew I had my own business, didn't you?"

"Sure, I knew about the shop," I said. But the truth was, I knew only a few vague details. Most of what I'd heard from Mom and Dad was how my aunt "dabbled"—dropped out of college, drifted around Europe, then returned to the States to write her memoirs, raise miniature pigs, sell real estate.

I rubbed Archie's cheek. "What would I do in the shop?"

"Oh, learn things, hopefully. Keep your old aunt company, mostly."

"Sure," I said. After all, hanging out with Aunt Shelby was the whole point of the summer, wasn't it? "But you aren't *old*."

"Say that again," she replied, and she laughed, sounding almost just like my mom.

False Unicorn

YOU MIGHT THINK THAT WITH ALL HER SIMMER-
ing pots in the kitchen, Aunt Shelby liked to cook. But
she didn't, at least most of the time. That night we ordered
sausage pizza for supper, and the next morning we had
frozen waffles for breakfast. I poured maple syrup on
mine; Aunt Shelby smothered hers in pineapple salsa and
sipped wildflower strawberry mango tea with two gobs
of honey.

I didn't know how to dress for Herb 'n' Renewal, so I
just wore jeans and my Camp Sunflower Hill tee. (Aunt

Shelby wore a baggy blue dress with a purple fringed shawl, but she didn't tell me to change my outfit, so I guessed she was okay with it.) We walked about a half mile to her store, which I'd imagined would be another version of her cottage: messy, a little smelly, and creaky.

But I was wrong. Herb 'n' Renewal gleamed. That's the only word for it. It was a small shop, but it had floor-to-ceiling shelves filled with jars of oils, powders, dried leaves, and capsules, all labeled and lined up in alphabetical order. The floor was spotless white, and all the surfaces—the counters, the stepladders, even the ceiling fan—were painted shiny green.

"Nice, huh?" Aunt Shelby asked proudly. "It's doing gangbusters too. Next I'm thinking of opening a sister shop called Herb 'n' Legend. That'll be more about crystals and incense you smell to enhance your whatever. Anyhow, I need investors, so I've brought it up with your dad. But between you and me, buttercup, he doesn't seem into it."

"Really?" I said politely.

"Yeah. I hate to say it, but your dad is too much of a linear thinker."

She took off her shawl and draped it over the back of a chair. Almost immediately a wind chime tinkled, and a mom-aged woman came in to buy some kind of tea with a spooky-sounding name. Then an older woman bought vitamins and foot lotion. Five minutes later, a blond woman in a fancy pink tennis outfit entered the store.

"Still no luck," the woman told Aunt Shelby, then burst into tears.

"Oh, Tara," Aunt Shelby said in a soothing voice. "It'll happen. I know it will."

"But I really thought this was the month!" Tara cried.

"I know you did. You just have to keep up our approach." She handed Tara a tissue and turned to me. "Tara, this is my niece, Amalia."

"Lia," I corrected her.

Aunt Shelby squeezed my shoulder. "Lia's staying with me this summer. Her mom died in a car accident. My big sister."

"Oh, how awful," Tara said, dabbing her eyes with the tissue.

"It truly was. The other driver should *rot*." Aunt Shelby sighed. "Anyway, I'm showing Lia the ropes here. Hope you don't mind."

Tara shook her head, obviously not interested in me at all. "The thing is, Shelby, I did exactly what you said—"

They talked about herbs, adjusting amounts, maybe subtracting one, adding another. Aunt Shelby took some powder out of a jar, weighed it on a shiny silver scale, and the woman paid. Then they hugged, and Tara left, tinkling wind chimes on the way out.

"Poor thing," Aunt Shelby said. "She wants a baby so badly, but it's just not happening for her."

I stared at my aunt. "You're giving her medicine?"

"Not *medicine*." Aunt Shelby smiled.

"What's in those jars, then?"

"Natural botanicals. Licorice root, false unicorn root—"

"FALSE UNICORN ROOT?"

"That's just its name, Lia. It's also called helonias, blazing star, and fairy wand. Native Americans have been using it for years."

"And you're telling her that if she takes that"—I waved at the jars—"*stuff*, she'll get pregnant? How do you know what to tell her to take? Or how much? I mean, you're not Native American. *Or* a doctor."

She turned on her computer. "Lia, you sound just like your dad."

"Well, he's my father." I started to feel sweaty, even though the grass-green ceiling fan was swishing overhead. "Why *shouldn't* I sound like him?"

"Listen, buttercup," Aunt Shelby said, sighing. "I do a lot of reading, especially about women's health issues. I attend seminars and webinars. I keep up with these things, okay? And of course I trust my intuition."

"But what if you're wrong? I mean, that woman believes you."

"You think I was *lying* to her?" Aunt Shelby's eyes were big. She seemed shocked that I would be challenging her.

I couldn't look at her face. "No. Not lying, but—"

"But what, then?"

I shook my head.

"Let me tell you something, Lia. These are genuine treatments. Centuries of wisdom handed down from various cultures. The Mesoamericans, the Native Americans, the ancient Chinese—"

"Can I go to the beach now?" I blurted.

She blinked. "Sure. If that's what you'd rather do, absolutely." She reached into a bag and handed me a key. "Let yourself into the house, change into your suit, and be sure to lock up. The beach is down the road in the other direction. Oh, and if you take a towel, hang it on the porch when you get back."

"Okay, thanks." I slipped the key in my jeans pocket.

If the wind chimes tinkled on my way out, I didn't hear them.

Tanner Than You

BUT I DIDN'T GO BACK TO AUNT SHELBY'S TO change. It wasn't like I was desperately longing to put on a bathing suit; all of mine were plain, boring one-pieces from last summer, and I looked like a third grader in them, anyway. Plus, I was so mad and confused that I just felt like walking straight to the beach. And to keep walking once I got there.

Why did I ever want to come here? I scolded myself. *Aunt Shelby is nuts. And if she isn't nuts, she's just a big fake. What business does she have telling Tara how to have a baby? If Tara wants to have a baby and she can't get pregnant for some reason, she should talk to a doctor, or to an actual herbologist-type person. Not to my aunt, who used to sell real estate and keep miniature pigs.*

Maybe I should have just gone to camp, I thought as I stepped onto the beach. I tugged off my sneakers, stuffing my socks into my pockets. Then I rolled up my jeans so they looked like capris. *I can't possibly talk to Aunt Shelby about my nonexistent period. She'll probably just give me false unicorn root. What a name. As opposed to real unicorn root, hahaha. I should tell Marley about that when I see her in September. Maybe if we wave a "fairy wand" we'll stop being Least Developed!*

Oh, and the way Aunt Shelby told Tara about my mom. Talking about the Accident as if it were gossip, or some kind of girl-talk chitchat. Talking about it in front of me, *as if it didn't even matter what I was feeling—*

"Hey, watch it!"

Just then I realized I'd stepped on a beach towel—and almost on the girl lying on it. She was seriously tan, with long, streaky blond hair, and she was wearing a neon orange bikini, the sort I'd never wear for five minutes, even in a private dressing room. But she looked great in it, as great as Jules would have, probably: Her chest filled out the top part without spilling over, her waist was small, and her stomach was flat. I guessed she was about as old as Nate, fourteen or fifteen, although it's not like I knew a bunch of teen girls to compare her to.

"Sorry," I muttered.

She glared at me. "Watch where you're walking, okay?" She turned to a darker-haired girl in a pink bikini who had earbuds on and was lying on a towel beside her. "I am *so sick* of tourist season, and it's only June," Orange Bikini announced.

"I'm not a tourist," I protested.

"You're not? You *look* like one."

I could feel myself blushing.

"You're all red," said Pink Bikini in an accusing sort of voice. "Want some sunscreen?"

I didn't know what else to do, so I took the tube and began smearing my arms. "Thanks," I said.

Suddenly something smacked my back. I spun around. A Frisbee.

"Hey, sorry," a guy called. He started walking toward us, the most gorgeous male human I'd ever seen in my entire life. Dark, wavy hair, golden skin, a smooth, muscled chest above navy blue beach trunks. I smeared the sunscreen on my face, because I knew I was blushing again.

"Tanner, watch where you're throwing that thing," Orange Bikini scolded him. "You hit this girl just now."

The way she said it, it was like "little girl."

"I'm okay," I said quickly.

"You sure?" Tanner said.

My heart boinged. You know, like in a cartoon, when someone's heart springs out of their chest? Because compared to this Tanner person, the boy I liked at school—Graydon Hatcher—resembled a toddler.

And Tanner was looking *right at me*. "Don't mean to scare away tourists," he said, grinning.

"I'm not a tourist." Now I was starting to get annoyed. "My aunt lives here."

"In Benchley?" Pink Bikini said. "Who's your aunt?"

"Shelby Heywood. She owns that shop in town, Herb 'n' Renewal . . . ?"

"Shelby's your aunt?" Tanner said. "Cool."

"You know her?"

He laughed. "Yeah, right. Not me."

"Then how do you—"

"Tanner, take that Frisbee away," Orange Bikini ordered. "We're not your target practice."

"Later," he said. He ran off to join some other kids playing volleyball.

Pink Bikini shaded her eyes at me. "Not to rush you or anything, but are you done with that sunscreen?"

"Oh, sure," I said. "Thanks for letting me borrow it."

"No prob," she said, as she and Orange Bikini stuck ear-buds back in their ears and stretched out lazily on their towels.

For the next week or two, Aunt Shelby and I didn't mention our fight, and as long as we didn't talk about the fake expert stuff, everything was fine between us. Sometimes it was even better than fine, like when she put on her ancient CDs and taught me to eighties-dance to Cyndi Lauper, Janet Jackson, and Madonna. Or when she took me out for "real Maine ice cream" one night and we traded cones halfway through, then both got seconds. Or when she showed me old photo albums of Mom and her as little kids and told me stories about how they made snow forts and caught frogs and shared chicken pox.

But every morning she ate a frozen waffle and fed the cats, then strolled to her store without inviting me to "hang out." And as soon as she was gone, I grabbed my book and ran to the beach to collect shells and sea glass.

Also, I have to admit, I was hoping for a Tanner sighting.

I knew it was stupid. I knew that even if I saw him, it wouldn't mean anything. He was about Nate's age, I guessed—in other words, about two years too old for me. Plus, he was probably a dope, the kind of guy who never read books. *Tanner.* What kind of name was that? It was more like a boast: *Dude, I'm tanner than you. Than you'll* ever *be.*

But I still wanted to spot him on the beach, with his stupid Frisbee. Don't ask why.

Also, I was wondering how he knew Aunt Shelby.

One day a couple of weeks later, in the middle of July, Aunt Shelby handed me two envelopes. They had both been sent to my home address, and Dad had forwarded them to Aunt Shelby.

The first one was from Abi.

Dear Lia,

I'm really, really mad at you for just running off like that in the parking lot without an explanation!!! None of us knew what to think! But then your dad told my mom that you wanted to stay with your aunt this summer. (My mom knows your aunt from when they were kids. You knew that, right?) Well, I hope you're having a fun time, because we are!!! I think I'm in <3 with a jr lifeguard named Nick! Also, we're playing this amazing game called Truth or Dare, which we'll do with you when we get home.

WRITE BACK OR I WILL STAY MAD.

XOXOX,

Abi

PS. I got my pd about a week after Mak.
U R NEXT (or Marley).

The other letter was from Marley. Although it wasn't really a letter—it was a drawing she made of a turtle. No explanation (*Today in art camp we did drawings of turtles!*), no note (*Dear Lia, How's your summer going?*), just the turtle drawing. It was a really nice picture, though. I decided to put it on a shelf in my room so I could look at it.

That evening Aunt Shelby made lasagna for dinner. She said it had a mystery ingredient and dared me to guess what it was. I told her I had no idea.

"C'mon, guess," she said.

"I'm drawing a blank. Garlic?"

"Of *course* it has garlic. Guess again."

"Oregano? Basil?"

"Cinnamon," she said triumphantly.

"Huh," I said. "Doesn't cinnamon usually go in desserts?"

"Well, the Aztecs used it in all sorts of things," she said, as if that were even a sane answer.

We both ate the lasagna. I thought I could taste the

cinnamon now that she'd mentioned it, but maybe it was just my imagination.

Finally, after about five minutes of me being unable to come up with conversation, Aunt Shelby said, "So, Lia. You got some mail today?"

"Yep," I said. I suddenly had this vision of my aunt snatching the letters, and I didn't want to explain the "U R NEXT" business. So I decided to distract her. "You know the mom of one of them. Valerie Franco?"

She grunted. "Yeah, Val. I remember her. Loudmouth. Big boobs."

"Aunt Shelby!"

"Well, she had 'em in high school for four years. It wasn't exactly a secret."

"She's an amazing cook," I said, struggling with some mozzarella. "She's helped us so much since the Accident."

Aunt Shelby made a face. "Back then she was a classic Mean Girl. What's her daughter like?"

"Abi? She's sort of our leader."

Aunt Shelby made another face.

"And she's really generous," I added. "She cares about her friends more than anything."

"Uh-huh. Tell me about your other friends."

"Well," I said, thinking. "Julianna—we call her Jules— is really sweet. She has an older sister who gives her clothes and stuff, so she's into fashion. Makayla's an incredible swimmer, and she plays the flute, and I think she's going to be president one day. Marley's an amazing artist."

"Sounds like a great bunch." Aunt Shelby pushed Brunhilda off her lap. "And which one are you?"

"Me?"

"In the group. What's *your* identity?"

I thought for a few seconds. Maybe it sounds weird, but I'd never thought of myself as the X in the group, or the Y person. "I'm the nice one, I guess."

Aunt Shelby studied me. "What does *that* mean, exactly?" she asked sharply.

"I'm the one everybody trusts with secrets. I'm a good listener. I stop fights. And I never fight with anyone."

"Huh," Aunt Shelby said, as if she'd never heard the concept of "nice" before. "So why aren't you with these friends for the summer, if you never fight?"

I shook my head. I knew this was my chance to tell my aunt everything—about camp, and undressing in the cabin, and how Abi just got her "pd," leaving only Marley and me. But right then I couldn't.

So I said, "It's a little complicated."

"In other words, you're fighting." She picked up a stringy piece of mozzarella with her fingers, watched it stretch, then ate it.

"We aren't," I protested. "My friends are all awesome. I don't know what I'd do without them."

"Yeah? Well, if that's true, you're lucky. I know *I* didn't feel that way when *I* was twelve. And you're making friends here on the beach?"

I sipped some water. "I'm mostly collecting shells and stuff. And reading."

"All day? No social interaction *at all*?"

The truth was: *Yes, Aunt Shelby. If you don't count Tanner and the Two Bikinis, I'm having* no *social interaction* at all. But if I told her that, she'd probably force me to come back to the store to witness her selling powdered unicorn horns, or whatever stuff she kept in those lined-up jars.

"Well, I met a boy," I admitted. "Once. He isn't a friend or anything—"

Her eyes widened. "Yeah? What's his name?"

"I don't remember. Tanner, I think."

"Oh, sure, Tanner Clayborne. Nice kid. He'll be a freshman at the local high school. His mom's a steady customer."

"Of yours?"

"Don't look so shocked, Lia. There are plenty of women around here who rely on my expertise. And in fact, Caroline Clayborne's become a good friend." Aunt Shelby stood up from the table to put her plate in the sink. "But I've been wondering something, niecelet. If you're at the beach every day, how come I never see you washing out any bathing suits?"

I felt my cheeks burn. "I just wear regular clothes to the beach."

"You mean those jeans? You didn't bring any suits from home?"

"No, I did, but they're all . . ." I couldn't finish the sentence. The problem wasn't the suits. It was how I looked in them. How I felt in them.

I chewed my thumb cuticle.

"Hey," Aunt Shelby said brightly, in a "girl talk" sort of voice. "Would you like to go shopping together? Not even just for bathing suits. For things maybe your dad doesn't know how to buy you. Like the right kind of underwear."

"I don't need any new underwear."

"Sure you do! And I know this great place two towns over, Winnie's Intimates. Winnie's actually a customer of mine, and also a close friend. She has a schnauzer."

Oh sure, I'll buy a bra from her, since she has a schnauzer.

"No, thank you," I said. I sipped some water.

"Why not? You mean you don't need to because you're boobless?"

I almost spat out the water.

"Aw, come on," Aunt Shelby said. "So you're a little behind in that department. Big deal. It's nothing but genetics, anyway! Your mom and I were both boobless until seventh grade. And you're going into seventh this year, am I right?"

I nodded.

"Then you'll definitely need back-to-school bras. It'll be fun! We could make an outing of it—first Winnie's, then lunch at Lulu's Lobster Shack."

"Aunt Shelby," I said firmly. "That sounds very nice, but I can just go bra shopping with my friends. At the mall. Val takes us all the time."

It was the truth, too. Val did drive us to the mall, like, once a month, sometimes specifically to go to Shy Violet's, a store that sold all kinds of underwear things. But I never went on those days—I couldn't imagine actually *buying* anything in there. Besides, I didn't want to undress in front of my friends.

I could tell Aunt Shelby felt disappointed that I'd turned her down, and for a second I felt sorry. But the thought of bra shopping with her was horrific. She'd probably discuss my boobless chest with Winnie right in front of me. In front of the schnauzer, too. It would be worse than a camp cabin.

Although hearing that Mom was flat at my age—that felt nice to know somehow. It made me feel closer to her, in a funny sort of way.

But at the same time, when I got into bed that night, it made me miss her even more.

Blueberry Pancakes

EVERY SUMMER GOES TOO FAST, IN MY OPINION. Even the kind of sticky summer where the weekdays and weekends basically just melt together.

But one weekend stood out, the time Dad and Nate drove up for a visit, and we ate crabs and corn on the cob and I introduced them to all the cats. Nate wasn't too interested, but Dad's favorite was Escobar; when he crumpled a wad of paper and threw it across the living room, Escobar fetched it for him over and over.

Before they drove back to Maplebrook, they pulled me aside.

"So how's it going up here?" Dad asked quietly.

"Okay," I said.

Nate poked me. "She's not making you eat toenail fungus?"

"Oh, we eat it all the time," I answered. "Fungus fondue. Fungus upside-down cake. Fungus à la mode."

My brother grinned. "Fungus pizza. Deep-fried fungus with fungus gravy."

"Fungus sorbet. General Tso's toenail fungus."

"All right, you two," Dad said, smiling a little. "But seriously, Lee-lee, if you want to come home—"

For a second I thought about it. But none of my friends would be home for weeks, and Maine wasn't terrible. I loved all the cats. Aunt Shelby was Aunt Shelby—but sometimes she could be fun. And there were times when her eyes lit up and her voice crackled in the middle of a sentence; that's when she reminded me of Mom.

"No, I'm fine," I insisted. "Really, Dad."

Another weekend Aunt Shelby took me on a seal-sighting boat, which I loved. We also went bicycling a couple of times with her "man friend," Todd, and picked blueberries along the side of the road.

During the week I mostly read Book Two of HiberNation

and hung out with the cats, or I walked on the beach and collected shells and sea glass. I thought I saw Tanner once or twice from a distance, and I definitely saw Orange Bikini a few times. But she pretended not to recognize me when I said hello to her at the snack bar, so I decided she was a snot. And anyway, she was in high school.

A few times a youngish red-haired woman wearing a UMass tee started a conversation with me as I searched for seashells. She told me her name was Yazmin and that she was studying marine biology in college. But she didn't want to talk about the beach, or the seals, or the shells, or even the sea glass I'd slipped into my jeans pocket. Instead she asked me about my book, my friends at home, who I was hanging out with in Benchley.

I thought it was a little odd but not creepy. Even so, I tried to keep away from her as much as I could. There weren't a whole lot of other people on the beach, so the ones who showed up every day, like Yazmin, were hard to avoid.

It was an okay summer, really. But I was lonely, and also a teeny bit bored.

Although three major things happened. The first was that Aunt Shelby took me bra shopping. Or to be precise: She *tricked* me into going, since she knew exactly how I felt on that subject.

One Sunday morning in early August she announced

that she "needed blueberry pancakes"—not any kind, but the specific ones they made at the Hummingbird Café two towns over, in Wheatly. And she insisted I needed some too, even though I'd already had waffles for breakfast.

We drove there in the pickup truck. Just as we were pulling into the small parking lot behind the Hummingbird Café, a woman with a small gray dog came running over to us, waving. Her hair was puffy in an eighties sort of way, and she wore a leopard-print top with a too-deep V-neck.

"Perfect timing," she told Aunt Shelby. "I was just taking Mothball out to do his business."

"No rush. This is Lia." Aunt Shelby turned to me, smiling. "Lia, this is Winnie, my friend who owns the bra store."

"I sell *intimates,* not just bras," Winnie corrected her. "Panties, shapewear, slips, camis, hosiery—"

A truck roared by, and now she was shouting.

"—and I'm having my big August sale now, so everything is forty percent off. So that's perfect timing too!"

She was beaming at me. So was Aunt Shelby.

I stared at them both.

"Wait," I said. "I thought—"

"And afterward we can go have pancakes." Aunt Shelby patted my knee. "Winnie isn't usually open on Sundays. She's doing it as a special favor. Isn't that sweet of her?"

I refused to answer.

We waited for Mothball to finish his "business," and then Winnie led us around the corner to her store. I was furious at my aunt for tricking me like this, but at least we'd be the only customers, I told myself. At least my humiliation would be semiprivate.

"All right, then, chickpea," Winnie said, waving me over to a three-way mirror. "Don't look so scared. I don't bite. Tape measure time!"

"Can I please use the bathroom first?" I begged.

"Sixty seconds," Aunt Shelby replied, pointing to her watch. "Hurry."

I don't know how long I was in there, but I took longer than sixty seconds, on purpose. When I came out, I could hear Shelby saying the words "cell phone" and "imbecile." As soon as they noticed me, they flashed big fake grins.

"And here she is, Princess Lia," Winnie exclaimed.

"You mean Leia, if that's a Star Wars reference," I muttered.

"Oh? It's spelled different?" Before I could answer, Winnie wound the tape measure around my chest. "Because I'm hopeless at spelling. Fortunately, in my line of work, I need just a few—stand still, chickpea—letters: A, B, C, D. Although one day last month a new customer walked in, and I swear, Shel, she was a size G. I had to place an *extra-special* order." Winnie scribbled something on a

Post-it. "You're like a skinny little bird, aren't you, Lia?"

"She eats like a horse," Aunt Shelby said, as if I weren't standing right there.

"And I *do* eat like a bird, and just *look* at me!" Winnie giggled. "Why don't you take the fitting room, Lia, and get yourself undressed. I'll be just a mo."

"Mo?" I said innocently. "What's a mo?"

Aunt Shelby gave me a warning eyebrow.

I went into the fitting room, a small curtained closet that smelled like leftover perfume. Why was it suddenly so important to Aunt Shelby that I get a bra? Had something happened this summer? I mean, to me?

I took off all my clothes, examining myself in the full-length mirror.

The answer was: No.

I was still as flat as a board. No waist. No hips. I was a straight line from my head to my toes. You could use me as a yardstick. Or a flagpole.

Also, I was still completely hairless on my legs. Under my navel. Under my arms. I guess you could call me bald, except for my head.

As long as I was taking inventory, I checked for symptoms. No zits on my face. No oil in my hair. No bloat in my belly. No cramps.

And mood swings? Irritability?

Nah.

I was still The Nice One. Nice to everyone, all the time. Even though my aunt made me want to kick something. Especially right at this mo.

Suddenly, the curtain swished.

I yelped.

But it was just Mothball, who sniffed my ankles (which probably smelled like cats), and ran out.

I put my shorts back on.

"All set there, Princess Lia?" Winnie called.

I wrapped my T-shirt around my chest. "Yep."

"Then open up," Winnie said cheerfully. "I've brought you some beautiful bras in all different styles, to give us an idea of what you're looking for."

"I'm not looking for anything." I opened the curtain just enough for her to shove an armload at me. Maybe twenty-five bras on these doll-size plastic hangers.

Whoa. They expected me to try on *all* of these?

Obviously, I wouldn't. There was just no way! And besides, most of these bras I could reject right away. For having rhinestones, fancy lace, polka dots, tropical flowers, padding.

Padding! I couldn't believe it. Aunt Shelby had said

booblessness was "no big deal." We were "late bloomers." It was all "genetics." So I totally did *not* get why she'd give me bras to fake looking *bigger*.

Plus, she was supposed to be all Natural Botanicals, Centuries of Wisdom, blah, blah, blah. So did she think in ancient Peru, Inca women put on fake boobholders every morning? What did they pad their bras with—dandelion fluff? Herbs and spices?

Also, some of these padded bras had underwire. Like to push your boobs upward. Correction: to push the *padding* upward, toward your chin.

Mom *never* would have bought me bras with chin cushions. She was all into sports bras for jogging. She cared about health and fitness, not about fake upward-pointing boobs and rhinestones. And if she were here with me right now, helping me find a bra that made any *sense*—

"What do you think, muffin? Aren't they pretty?" Winnie cooed.

"Mm-hmm," I said.

"Let me know if you need any help trying on."

"Okay, thanks."

Well, if I subtract all the rejects, that leaves me five I should probably try on, just to get out of here, I told myself. I grabbed one of the five finalists—a plain pink unpadded one with a little bow in the center, the sort of thing I would have liked if I was six years old and playing Underwear Dress-up.

I put my arms through the straps. Then I tried to fasten it in the back.

It didn't work.

Wait. Seriously?

I took a deep breath and tried again.

And again.

Nope. Still couldn't do it.

I craned my neck to look behind myself in the mirror, but even with this backward view, I still couldn't get both hooks to catch on both of the hook thingies. If they caught on *one* of the hook thingies, it was the *wrong* one. Once I got Hook A to catch on Hook Thingy A, but it came out just as I started working on Hook B. No matter how many times I tried, it was like I was playing with a sadistic crane machine at an arcade, the kind that took your quarter and refused to give you a prize.

"Need some help in there?" Winnie asked sweetly.

"No, I'm good," I said, giving up.

"You know, niecelet, Winnie's a bra expert," Aunt Shelby said. "Women come from up and down the coast for her expertise."

"Oh, Shelby," Winnie said. "*You're* the one they come to see!"

"Well, sometimes."

"Always! *You're* the expert! Lia, did you realize your aunt was a famous women's health guru?"

I grabbed another bra, a blue one. This one was considerate enough to attach in the front, but the straps were so loose they were flopping off my shoulders. There had to be a way to make them tighter, right? I tugged and tugged, but I couldn't figure it out. *Why was this bra stuff so ridiculously complicated? And what is the point of wearing training bras if they don't train you how put these stupid things on?*

"How's it going in there?" Aunt Shelby called.

"Great," I said.

"Want any help?"

"*No!*"

"Okay, chickpea, so we're waiting for the fashion show," Winnie said.

What? No way! I threw on my T-shirt, grabbed the five finalists, and yanked open the curtain. "Sorry, but I've already decided on these. If it's okay to get five."

Aunt Shelby beamed at me. "Of course it's okay!"

"And at forty percent off, they're a steal," Winnie told my aunt.

I watched my aunt take out her purse and pay, even though I knew I'd never wear any of them, just stuff them into a drawer or something. And not only because they were impossible to put on, but on principle—the principle being, You should be honest with your niece and not trick her into buying personal stuff she didn't need and didn't want.

Also, you shouldn't embarrass her in front of strangers and their schnauzers.

Also, you shouldn't promise her blueberry pancakes and totally forget about them after shopping.

Something to Talk About

THE SECOND THING THAT HAPPENED WAS: ONE rainy afternoon, Demon Spawn showed up at the beach house with a bloody gash on her cheek. She was still not quite used to me, so to clean her face, I basically had to trap her in the corner of the kitchen and fling some cold water at her while she hissed at me. Aunt Shelby had taken her cell phone with her to the shop, which meant I didn't have any way to call her. So finally I grabbed my raincoat and hurried over to Herb 'n' Renewal.

When I got there, Aunt Shelby was leaning on her

counter, drinking tea with a customer in a blue hoodie. A youngish, red-haired woman who smiled at me as she looked up from her mug. My insides dropped when I realized it was Yazmin, the person who'd been asking those nosy questions on the beach.

"You know each other?" I squeaked, dripping rain on Aunt Shelby's clean white floor.

Yazmin glanced at my aunt, whose smile was too wide.

I waited for an answer.

"It's a very small town," Aunt Shelby finally said, with just a little bit too much cheeriness.

Yazmin zipped up her hoodie. "Well, you guys, gotta run, so . . . ," she said. "Nice to see you again, Lia."

I watched her flee the store. Then I turned to Aunt Shelby.

"To what do I owe the honor of your presence?" she asked, pretending to clean the counter with a sponge.

"Demon Spawn was in a catfight, probably," I said. "You should take her to the vet. Can I ask you a question?"

"Sure." She didn't look at me.

"Has that woman—Yazmin, if that's her real name—been spying on me? At the beach?"

Aunt Shelby continued the pretend cleaning. "Why do you think that?"

"Because I see her all the time. She's been asking me all

these questions. She never seems to have anything else to do. And she said she was studying marine biology, but she never talks about it. Ever."

Aunt Shelby stopped cleaning. She took a breath. She sipped her tea. Then she rested her elbows on the counter and said, "All right, buttercup. You want the truth?"

I nodded.

"Then here it is. Yazmin came to me for a summer job, so I asked her to keep an eye on you. Not spy."

"What's the difference?"

"Oh, a big one, Lia. You were by yourself on the beach all day long. You don't have a cell phone, right? So you couldn't even call me in an emergency! I just wanted to make sure you were okay."

"I'm not a baby!"

"Right. And that's exactly *why* I wanted her to keep an eye on you."

"Huh? That doesn't make any—"

"Sweetheart, there are *teenage boys* on the beach. Haven't you noticed?"

My face burned. "Of course I've noticed! You think I wouldn't even—"

"And I don't trust teenage boys."

"You don't trust *me*."

"Lia, it's not about you." She sighed. "I owe it to your mom—"

"To hire a *spy?*"

"I wish you'd stop using that word."

"Why? Because it's true?"

The conversation went on like this, around and around, like a no-fun Ferris wheel. It finally ended when the shop closed for the day and Aunt Shelby drove Demon Spawn three towns over to the all-night animal hospital.

The next morning, when I got up, she'd already left for work.

The third thing that happened: A couple of nights after the Spy Incident, Aunt Shelby announced that she'd invited one of her "good friends" over for dinner. ("Don't worry, it's not Yazmin," she said. "I'm not worried," I muttered, because I was still mad at my aunt.) But my stomach was squirming anyway: Had she invited Winnie and her schnauzer? Were we going to discuss my boobless situation over lasagna? Debate the topic "Padding: Good or Incredibly Fake and Evil?"

Or even worse: Were they going to make me runway-model the five bras for them, so they could *offer comments?* ("Better? Or worse?") If so, I'd rather the "good friend" was Yazmin. The worst she'd do was get me to discuss my social life.

That night I wore one of Nate's old Maplebrook High School tees. He'd outgrown it, so I'd swiped it; on me it was enormous, which meant my chest wouldn't be available for Winnie's commentary.

Aunt Shelby frowned as I set the table. I guessed she thought I looked grungy in Nate's tee, and I knew I did, but she didn't say anything, and I didn't care. So what if I embarrassed her, I told myself. After the spying business, she deserved it.

At six fifteen there was a knock on the door.

"Would you get that, Lia?" Aunt Shelby called from the kitchen. I opened the door.

It was a smiling blond woman in a sleeveless blue dress. She had one of those mom-ponytails like the kind Val had, and she was holding a gloppy homemade-looking pie that was probably blueberry.

Just behind her, wearing a plaid shirt over a faded tee, was Tanner.

My heart boinged.

"Come in, come in," Aunt Shelby squealed behind me. "This is my darling niece, Lia. Lia, I want you to meet my good friend Caroline Clayborne, and I think you've already met her son, Tanner."

Tanner smiled. His teeth were very white, or maybe they just looked that way compared to his ridiculously tan skin. And his features were perfectly lined up, everything straight and parallel, like his face was drawn on graph paper.

"We've met?" he asked me, looking confused but still smiling.

My face burst into blushes. "Like, a few weeks ago. At the beginning of summer, I think. You threw your Frisbee at me. By mistake."

"I did? Well, sorry."

"You already apologized."

"Oh. Then sorry I apologized *again*."

Mrs. Clayborne and Aunt Shelby laughed, the way grown-ups laugh when they don't have anything to say. Then Mrs. Clayborne and her pie followed Aunt Shelby into the kitchen.

Leaving me in the living room with Tanner and four-sixths of the cats.

"Wow," he said, seating himself on the shredded chair. "Your aunt sure has a lot of cats."

"She fosters for Benchley Rescues. That's not all of them; there are two more. Escobar and Pashmina are hiding somewhere." I pretended to look under the love seat. While I was down there, I wiped my sweaty forehead with the hem of Nate's T-shirt.

TANNER WAS HERE FOR DINNER. WE WERE ALONE TOGETHER IN THE LIVING ROOM.

Finally I had to get up for air. "Nope, they're not under there," I said brightly.

He smiled again. "I hate cats."

"Really? I love them. I always wanted one, but my mom—"

As soon as I said the word "mom," I froze. I should never have brought her up. She wasn't just something to talk about.

"Allergies?" Tanner asked.

"Uh-huh. To cat fur." Which was probably a lie Mom had told me.

"So is Logan," Tanner said, nodding. "Her face blows up. I mean swells, not *kabooms*."

"Who's Logan?"

"Hey, I'll show you." He took his phone out of his pocket, scrolled thorough some stuff, then handed it to me. "That's her on the beach," he said proudly.

I stared at the photo. It was Orange Bikini. You could see her chest sticking out the top of her bra. *Cleavage*, which always sounded to me like the name of a disease. *Sorry to tell you this, madam, but you're suffering from a severe case of cleavage. Fortunately, we have antibiotics.*

I swallowed. "Your girlfriend?"

"Yeah. We just had our three-month anniversary. Isn't she hot?"

I gave him back the phone. "I guess," I said. "I wouldn't know."

He grinned so I could see his perfect teeth again. "You will when you grow up," he said.

Then he did something truly horrific. *He messed my hair.* Like I was a little kid. Or a puppy.

I almost bit him.

Aunt Shelby called us into the kitchen for supper. I don't know how I got through that dinner. Mrs. Clayborne kept asking me about school and Maplebrook and my friends, so basically I had to talk about how babyish I was. Tanner didn't say very much; he ate about half the entire serving bowl of veggie chili, so he really didn't have time to talk between bites, anyway. Finally he finished, gave a little burp into his napkin, then sent someone a text. I figured it was Orange Bikini, Whose Face Swelled Up from Cats (yay, cats!) and Who Was Snotty to Me Because She Thought I Was a Little Girl.

"Awesome chili," Tanner said, when he'd stopped texting.

"Thank you," Aunt Shelby said, bowing her head. "This time I added a mystery ingredient. Can you figure out what it is?"

"Cinnamon," I said.

"Nope."

"Ketchup?" Tanner asked.

"Nope. Although what a good idea; I might try that in the future."

Tanner smiled. You could tell he was proud of himself for thinking of ketchup. *What a dumbo,* I thought.

"Hmm," Mrs. Clayborne said, as if she were searching through her mental spice rack. "How about cumin?"

Aunt Shelby shook her braids. "*Maple syrup!* It really sets up the spices, don't you think?"

"Oh yes," Mrs. Clayborne said enthusiastically, although I might have seen her gag into her napkin.

They finally left around nine o'clock.

When the door closed, Aunt Shelby grinned at me. "So, Lia. I guess there *are* some nice teen boys around here, after all. Don't you think?"

I realized this was her way of apologizing.

But I didn't care. By then I was feeling like a messy blob of blueberry-pie filling.

"Aunt Shelby?" I said. "Can I ask you something?"

She put a hand on my shoulder. "Niecelet, you can ask me anything. Anytime."

"Can I go home now?"

My aunt opened her mouth like she was going to protest. But all she said was, "If that's what you want. Of course you can, Lia."

Souvenirs

THREE DAYS LATER, I WAS BACK IN MAPLEBROOK.
Dad didn't ask why I wanted to come home two weeks
early when none of my friends were back in town yet,
and I didn't explain. Even if he had asked, I'm not sure
what I would have said. *I went to Maine so I wouldn't
have to deal with girl stuff; I came home so I wouldn't
have to deal with Shelby.* Because the truth was my aunt
was the total opposite of my mom. Who knew how to
listen. Who didn't act judgy. And who would never have
hired a spy, or invited Tanner for dinner, or tricked me

into getting bras instead of blueberry pancakes.

Or stuffed the bras into my duffel bag *along with three more, the kind with the padding.* Aunt Shelby had obviously gone back to Winnie's Intimates on her own, without me, and said to Winnie something like, "Oh, I'm sure my little niecelet meant to buy these super-fake padded ones too and was just too shy to admit it!" And Winnie would have answered, "You're the expert, Shel—and at forty percent off, they're a steal!" Aunt Shelby must have decided it was simpler not to mention them to me, and just snuck them into my bag right before Dad came to drive me home. She'd even pinned a note to the pink bra with the little-girl ribbon in the center:

Dear Lia,

Even if you don't think you need these now, you will later. Heywood girls are late bloomers, but we're worth the wait!!

Here whenever you need me. Call anytime, and please visit again soon!!

So much love,

Aunt Shelby, Stinkbug, Pashmina, Escobar,
Doomhammer & Archie. Also Demon Spawn,
who is feeling much better now. ☺

When I read this note, I was so mad I felt like punching something. My aunt had zipped open my private bag, forced those extra stupid bras on me, maybe even snooped through my personal things, because she thought she "owed it" to Mom. Did she *ever once* consider *my* feelings? It was clear that the answer was no.

I tossed the bras—all *eight* of them now!—into my closet.

For the next two weeks Dad kept Nate and me busy with end-of-summer stuff—doctor checkups, dentist checkups, an expedition to the Maplebrook Mall for new sneakers. He even took me shopping for a few new tops and a couple of sweaters, which I thought was pretty nice of him. Although back-to-school shopping was one of those things that made me miss Mom extra hard, so I only pretended to be happy.

On the Wednesday before school was about to start, Marley came home from Chicago. She'd brought me a tiny Chicago Cubs pennant, so I gave her three pieces of sea glass—green, ice blue, and white. She went nuts thanking me for them and promised to draw them in different poses. Then she went on and on about all the fun stuff she did in art class, all the fun places she visited in Chicago, and all the fun things she did with her fun cousins. Finally she asked about my summer.

"Oh, you know," I said. "I mostly hung out on the beach. And read."

I saw her eyes change behind her glasses. I knew that look very well. She felt sorry for me.

" . . . and shopped with my aunt," I added.

"Yeah?" Marley said. "Like for what?"

"You know. Stuff I can't really do with my dad."

She blinked. "Oh, right," she said. "That."

The next day Abi, Jules, and Makayla returned from camp. I knew about the bus arriving in Maplebrook because I still had a copy of the camp schedule, and for a minute I actually considered meeting them in the parking lot. But I didn't.

That night Abi and Jules showed up at my house.

I screamed when I opened the door. They screamed back.

We stood there screaming.

Nate came running. "Lia, what's going—oh. Hey, Julianna. Did you have a nice summer?"

"Yeah," Jules said, smiling. All the screaming had turned her cheeks extra pink. "It was awesome. How was yours?"

"Not too bad, considering I was stuck here."

"Oh, poor Nate," Abi exclaimed. "My heart bleeds for you." She laughed loudly.

The three of us ran upstairs to my room. I immediately shut the door, and we all plopped on my bed. Abi looked browner than before. Taller, too, as if her body had been stretched after washing. (So I didn't see how Nate—or anybody else—could call her "fat" anymore. Not that she ever was.) She was wearing her long dark hair pulled tightly in a high side ponytail; that was a new style for Abi, and I wasn't sure how I felt about it, truthfully. I mean, it made her look older.

Jules looked the same as before the summer, except her blond hair was lightened by the sun, and her skin was scabby with old mosquito bites and faded poison ivy. Both of them were wearing tank tops that showed pink bra straps; both of them had fingernails polished sky blue.

"Omigod, we haven't been together in *ages*," Abi exclaimed. "I missed you *so much*, Lia! But you know I'm still mad at how you deserted us like that!"

"But you can't be," I protested. "I wrote you back, didn't I? You said you'd be mad if I *didn't*."

"You didn't write to *me*," Jules said, pouting.

"That's because I didn't have tons to report." I stopped myself; the last thing I wanted was more friend pity.

"Anyhow, I was kind of busy at my aunt's. Did you have a great time?"

"Haha, *did* we, Jules?" Abi teased. "Oh yeah, and we made something for you."

They both reached into the pockets of their shorts and pulled out lanyard thingies. One was red, white, and blue, and the other was yellow and green, our school colors.

I didn't know what to say. Lanyards were one of those things that were so important when you were at camp and kind of pointless once you were back in the real world.

"They're key chains," Abi explained.

"Or you could use them for other stuff," Jules said.

"But they're best as key chains," Abi insisted.

"They're so cool," I gushed. "Thanks."

But if Abi and Jules were giving me souvenirs, I had to give them something too, so I reached into a bin to scoop up more sea glass. It stung a little to give away so much of my newest collection, and who knew when I'd ever go back to Aunt Shelby's beach. But the sea glass seemed to be a good choice, anyway; they both went, "*Oooooh.*"

"So where's Makayla?" I asked, when they'd finished oohing.

Abi and Jules exchanged glances.

"What?" I said.

"It's . . . um, gotten slightly weird with her lately," Jules said. She scratched a scab on her shoulder.

"What do you mean by 'weird'?" I looked at Abi.

Abi sighed. "I'm only telling you about this because I trust you, Lia. You can't tell anyone else."

"Who would I tell?"

"I don't know. Marley?"

"I won't tell anyone if you don't want me to," I promised. "What happened?"

"Okay. So all summer I had this mega crush on this lifeguard named Nick."

"Junior lifeguard," Jules reminded her.

"And Makayla knew about it?" I asked.

Abi nodded. "Oh, definitely. And by the way, she's called Mak now."

"Mak?"

"Everybody in our cabin had to have a nickname," Jules explained. "I already have one, obviously, and nobody calls Abi 'Abigail,' so Makayla had to be Mak. Oh, and all the counselors were named after food. Like we had Cupcake, Lollipop, Snickers, Funyun—"

"Wait," I said, giggling. "'Funyun'?"

"*Anyway,*" Abi said loudly. "So on the last day of camp, when we were all at the lake, Mak kept showing off her swim-team strokes. To get Nick's attention. And it totally worked. He didn't pay one bit of attention to me; when he got on the bus, he didn't even say good-bye."

"Huh," I said. "Are you saying she was trying to steal him from you, Abi? Maybe she was just practicing for swim team."

"You want to know the truth, Lia? Mak is always so competitive with me! It got really, really bad this summer. It's like she has to be the best all the time, and she won't let me have *anything*." Abi's voice wobbled.

Jules put her arm around Abi's shoulder.

"Did you talk to her about it?" I asked.

"I tried! She just denied the whole thing. The worst part was that she didn't even *care* that she hurt my feelings." Abi sighed. "Oh, never mind, Lia. I didn't mean to talk about all this. I really just wanted to invite you to my sleepover this Saturday night. Can you come?"

"Sure," I said quickly.

"Yay!" Jules beamed at me. "Marley's coming too."

"But not—?"

"Of course I *invited* Mak, but who knows if she'll even come," Abi said. "It's totally up to her, you know?"

Then they both left, leaving the sea glass on my bed.

Truth or Dare

THAT SATURDAY AT FIVE-THIRTY, MARLEY showed up at my door wearing a Chicago Cubs jersey, blue gym shorts, and blue and red rubber bands on her teeth. We were walking over to Abi's together, which was definitely awkward, because Abi had told me not to tell "anyone" about the business with Makayla, and "anyone" included Marley. But then I realized that Abi and Jules had already invited Marley before they came to my house, so maybe they'd told her the whole Makayla story first.

Although I doubted it. It wasn't just because Abi had

said all that stuff about telling *me* because she trusted me. It was also because of a feeling I had, a feeling I didn't like to admit—that Marley was connected to the group through *me*. That the other girls didn't see her coolness the way I did. That she was sort of on the edge of things, like a moon that could slip out of orbit one day and just kind of drift away.

I worried: What would Marley think when we got to Abi's if Makayla wasn't there? Would Abi (and Jules) even give her any explanation? Or make up a lame excuse—*Mak said she had her period and just felt too bleh to see her best friends?*

But it turned out that I didn't need to worry about any of this. Because when Marley and I arrived at Abi's house, Makayla was already there, in the kitchen, sitting on a stool and eating cherry Twizzlers.

"No more braces!" she shouted as a greeting. "They came off yesterday, and now I can eat Twizzlers again, my long-lost loves!"

"That's so great!" I exclaimed. My eyes darted over to Abi, to see if I could detect any weirdness between them. But Abi was beaming.

So was Makayla. "Although I still have this stupid retainer, but I don't care! I don't care if I *turn into* a Twizzler!"

Abi, Jules, and Marley laughed.

Abi put her arm around Makayla's shoulder. "Careful, dahling. Or you'll end up like Ren!"

"Who's Ren?" Marley asked.

"Omigod," Makayla exclaimed. "This girl at camp? All she ate was ice cream and carrots, ice cream and carrots."

"Together?" Marley made a face.

"No, you dummy, one at a time. Ice cream, then nothing but carrots all day. Then more ice cream and a ton more carrots. And from all the carrots? Her skin actually turned *orange*."

"It literally did," Abi said, laughing. "She looked like she had a spray-on tan, except she picked the wrong shade."

"It's not funny," Jules said. But she was giggling.

"Girls, to me your friend sounds like she had some eating issues," Val commented. How much had she been hearing, I wondered, as Val turned off the oven and stacked some plates on the table for us. "I certainly hope *you* didn't eat like that this summer."

"Oh, don't worry about *us*," Makayla said, laughing. "We ate everything! And seconds! And thirds!"

"Omigod, that chocolate cake they had at camp." Jules gasped dramatically. "I'm going to starve without it, I swear."

Val smiled. "Yes, I heard about that cake from Abi, so I thought I'd make chocolate cupcakes for you girls for dessert. After pizza." She put one arm around Abi's shoulder and one arm around mine. "Oh, I missed my girls so much," she cried.

"We missed you too," Makayla said. Then she threw her arms around Val and squeezed the three of us, which made me feel like a limp piece of lettuce inside an overstuffed sandwich.

When we'd finished our pizza, Abi announced, "All right, dahlings, time for fun and games!"

Looking back at everything that happened, this probably should have been a giant neon warning sign for me. Seventh-grade girls don't do "fun and games" unless there's a trophy involved. At least, *we* didn't; all the girls I knew were ultra-competitive.

But I was just so glad to be back with my friends. They weren't even fighting anymore. We were having a sleepover at Abi's, the way we always did—pizza for supper, then one of Val's amazing desserts. And it was so nice how she let us bring the cupcakes upstairs to Abi's formerly pink bedroom, which was now black and white and full of so many clashing animal-skin patterns it made me kind of woozy.

The five of us sat cross-legged on the floor, trying not to get chocolate frosting on Abi's new white shag rug.

"Okay, so here's the game," Abi announced. "It's called Truth or Dare."

"Truth or Dare?" Marley repeated, licking some frosting off her pointer finger.

"We played it in camp this summer," Makayla explained. "It's the most fun ever. The way it works is—"

"You don't need to tell me," Marley interrupted. "I do it with my cousins. And I'm not sure."

"About what?"

"If it's such a good idea, frankly."

Makayla shrugged. "We played it with counselors. As a bonding thing."

"It's really fun, Marley," Jules said. "Don't worry."

"I'm not *worried*," Marley said. "I just don't know if I want to *play*."

Abi shrugged. "Fine. Then don't."

A secret conversation started then between Abi's eyes and Makayla's eyes. Jules's eyes might have been in on it too; I couldn't tell for sure.

"Hey, guys," I said, trying to sound casual. "Can you explain the rules to me? I've never played Truth or Dare."

(This wasn't a lie; I'd never played it before. I knew the rules, though; pretending not to was just a way to change the subject.)

"Okay, Lia," Abi said, happy that she could explain something. "So we sit in a circle, right? And let's say I start. I turn to the first person on my right, who in this case is the beauteous Mak—"

Makayla did a diva smile and wave.

"—and I ask her, truth or dare?"

"Truth, dahling," Makayla said, making a kissy face.

Abi slapped her arm. "Which means I get to ask Mak a question, which she has to answer truthfully. No topic is off-limits, okay? Because we're all best friends. So let's say I ask her, 'Who is your secret crush?'"

Uh-oh, I thought. *Here we go.*

"Well, it isn't Nick," Makayla declared. "Okay?"

Abi rolled her eyes and smiled.

"But you didn't answer the question, dahling," Jules reminded Makayla.

"Fine, dahling," Makayla said. "It's Sean."

"*EWW*," Abi shouted, and Jules said, "Seriously? You mean that gross CIT?"

"I thought he was cute," Makayla said. "In a bad-complexion sort of way."

I glanced at Marley. More camp talk that we didn't get. Was she starting to feel as left out as I did? And what was all this "dahling" stuff about?

I began chewing my thumb cuticle.

Makayla took a big bite of cupcake. "So anyway, Lia. I told my truth, and now I turn to the person sitting on my right."

"Who's me," Jules said. "And I choose dare."

Makayla grinned. You could see some frosting on her teeth. "You sure?"

"Totally. Bring it, Mak."

"You asked for it, Julesie." Mak looked at the ceiling for a few seconds. "Okay. I dare you to eat that cupcake with no hands."

Jules squealed. "I totally hate you," she told Mak.

Then she took a deep breath, put her arms behind her back like an Olympic speed skater, and gobbled up the cupcake, the entire thing, while all of us clapped and laughed. Even Marley, who apparently had decided to play.

Finally Jules looked up. She had frosting all over her mouth and her chin, and some gobs were sticking to her hair. "Victory," she announced, then ran into Abi's bathroom. We could hear her turn on the faucet full blast.

"What happens if you don't complete the dare?" I asked.

"Then you have to repeat the turn," Abi said. "Although if you're caught telling a lie, you're banished forever."

"Because truth is the *most important* part of the game," Makayla added.

Jules stepped out of the bathroom with a pink, chocolate-free face. "What did I miss?"

"Nothing, dahling," Abi said. "We were waiting for you." She turned to Marley. "Now it's your turn."

"Dare," Marley said immediately. She looked a little pale, I thought, but maybe that was from too much pizza.

Jules glanced at Abi. "You sure?"

Marley nodded.

Jules smiled as she plopped down again on the white rug. "Okay, here goes. Marley, I dare you to take off your bra and show us the label, so we can all see your bra size!"

I swallowed. Marley didn't even own a bra, and everyone knew it.

"No," Marley said.

Abi did a slow blink. "You refuse?"

"Right. I refuse."

"Then you have to leave."

"You mean leave the game?" I said, staring at Abi.

"I mean leave my house," Abi replied calmly. "That's the rule."

Marley was staring at a hole in one of her socks. She stuck her pointer finger in the hole and made it bigger.

"That's not fair," I protested. "Nobody ever said if you refuse a dare you have to go home. You should give Marley another chance."

Abi and Mak had their eye conversation again.

"Fine," Abi said. "Same dare. She has one more chance to accept, but that's it."

All of a sudden Marley jumped to her feet, reached under her Chicago Cubs jersey, wriggled a bit, and pulled out a pale blue bra through her sleeve. "30A!" she declared. "Are you happy now?"

Abi and Mak examined the label. They passed it to Jules, who offered it to me, but I didn't look.

"We're satisfied," Abi announced. "Okay, Marley. Now you get to ask Lia."

Marley snatched her bra from Jules and headed to the bathroom. "What if I don't want to ask Lia?"

"You can forfeit your turn, then."

"Great! Go ahead without me!"

Makayla shrugged. "All right, Lia, so which do you choose?"

"Truth," I said. I mean, all I had on under my top was one of those lame no-boob training bras. Marley had gone out and bought some real bras, apparently. Maybe in Chicago this summer—or after I'd lied to her about "shopping." It was weird she hadn't even mentioned it to me. Was she afraid I'd accuse her of copying, or something?

Mak, Jules, and Abi huddled. All of my saliva dried into dust.

Then Jules smiled sweetly. "So, Lia," she said. "Here's your question. Have you ever kissed a boy who wasn't your brother?"

"Oh, sure," I blurted.

Jules looked surprised but quickly recovered. "Who was it?"

"His name is Tanner. He's a freshman in high school. I met him this summer up in Maine."

"Seriously," Abi said. It was more of a comment than a question. "So what did he look like?"

"Incredibly cute. Brown eyes. Dark hair. Nice teeth." Which was all true.

"You just walked up to this strange boy and *kissed* him?" Makayla asked, her eyes wide.

"No, of course not. I met him when my aunt invited his family over for dinner." Also true. "And afterward we took a walk on the beach. And we kissed."

Which of course wasn't.

"On the *mouth?*" Jules was gaping.

"Yeah," I said.

"For how long?"

"I don't know. A minute, maybe?"

Makayla's eyebrows rose. "An *entire minute?*"

"Okay, no. More like twenty seconds, maybe. Or fifteen. I wasn't counting."

"Huh," Abi said. She glanced at Makayla. "Were your eyes closed?"

I nodded.

"Were his?"

"Yeah."

"How do you know that if your eyes were closed?"

I swallowed some saliva dust. "I mean, I assume they were. I'm not positive."

"So what did his lips taste like?" Jules asked.

"Chili. My aunt made veggie chili for supper. It was pretty good. Not too spicy. Although she *did* add some maple syrup—"

"Who pulled away first?" Makayla interrupted.

"Me. Although sort of both of us."

Makayla, Abi, and Jules looked at each other. Something was communicated, a secret silent code you could decipher only if you went to their camp, swam in their lake, got stung by their mosquitoes.

Finally Abi took a tiny bite of cupcake. "And was there an exchange of spit?"

Jules and Mak both went, "*Eww.*"

"What's wrong?" Abi asked, laughing. "It's a totally fair question."

"You think so?" Now Marley was back, smoothing the front of her jersey. "Because in the version of Truth or

Dare I played with my cousins, you weren't allowed to ask a bunch of follow-up questions."

"Well, this is *our* version," Makayla said.

"But it's still Truth or Dare, right? Not A Million Truths We Get to Keep Asking Lia About. So I'm pretty sure by now it's Abi's turn. Isn't it?"

Abi did her laugh. "Fine," she said. "I choose dare. Lia, go ahead, dare me."

Everyone looked at me, waiting.

I was too jittery to come up with a good one. So I dared Abi to sing a Disney song out the window, and she screamed "Let It Go" at the top of her lungs.

The whole time I kept replaying our game and what I'd just said, wishing I could somehow hit the Delete key.

Nothing's Off-Limits

I'D LIKE TO TELL YOU THAT I DIDN'T SLEEP THAT night, and that all of Sunday I squirmed and blushed when I thought about the lie I'd told my friends. But here's the truth—by the next morning I felt proud of myself. The tiny green bud of the lie—*I kissed Tanner*—had bloomed into a gorgeous pink flower overnight, a great big peony I could keep in a vase in front of me and take whiffs of whenever I felt left out of the conversation. *I kissed Tanner* wasn't the truth as a statement of What Actually Happened to Me That Summer, but it was a different kind of truth—a statement of What Was Going on Inside My Brain, how all of a sudden I could come up with details (the walk on the beach, the fifteen-second kiss, the closed eyes). I mean, I'd never even *thought* of stuff like that before, ever. Not about myself, anyway. So I felt excited, and maybe a little bit scared, about my new power.

Seventh grade started the following Tuesday. After the unfun summer I'd had, I wasn't even dreading school all that much. And the first day wasn't even that terrible— all of my friends except Marley were in my PE class, and Marley and Mak were both in my homeroom. And my teachers seemed decent, with the exception of Mrs. Crawley for math, whose nose job was totally distracting, and Mr. Halloran for homeroom and English, whose breath stank like onions and tuna fish.

I also secretly celebrated that my crush, Graydon, was in all my classes. After seeing Tanner up close this summer, I had to admit that Graydon wasn't what you'd call "typical" cute. He was short, for one thing. Also, his wrists were bony and his glasses were always smudged. But he was incredibly smart and funny, and I liked the way his hair curled around his ears. A few times last year he let me borrow his homework. Once he asked me to dance at a boy-girl party Abi had in her basement; I stepped on his toes a couple of times and he didn't even tease me about it.

Anyway, on our first day back, my friends and I played Truth or Dare again in the lunchroom. I had watered the Tanner Flower so much over the weekend that by lunch period it was almost a bouquet: I'd decided what his cheek felt like and how his hair smelled, what we talked about before kissing, how we strolled on the sand afterward. (*I'd taken off my sandals; the damp sand cooled my toes, and the cold tide nipped at my ankles. Oh, right—and I even found some sea glass.*)

In fact, I was so prepared for follow-up kiss questions that I barely paid attention to the game. Makayla asked Jules the grossest thing she ever ate (answer: snot, which her little brother sneaked into the peanut butter); Abi asked Makayla if she'd ever peed in the pool (answer: yes, twice); Jules asked Abi if she'd ever cheated on a test (answer: yes, once on a math test, when she'd copied two of Graydon's answers).

And then Abi turned to me. "Truth or dare?"

"Truth," I said right away. My heart was pounding. This time I was ready.

"Okay. So here's your question, Lia: Did you get your period yet?"

"What?" I stared.

"You know. Did you *start*?"

"Men-stru-a-ting," Makayla enunciated, as if she were the voice-over in one of those health class videos.

"Are you really asking her that?" Marley demanded. "Isn't that personal?"

"We told you the rules," Abi replied, not even looking at Marley. "Nothing's off-limits."

"Yeah, I know, but—"

"Actually, I did," I blurted. "Over the summer."

Jules squealed. "Really, Lia? Why didn't you tell us?"

"It's kind of a painful topic."

"Oh, I knowww," Jules said, making sympathetic eyes. "You had killer cramps?"

"No, I mean painful embarrassing." I started twirling the corners of my napkin. "Because it happened with Tanner. On the beach. We were walking, and all of a sudden I just . . . you know, felt it."

Marley glanced up at me.

"At first I didn't know what it was," I continued. "My leg was wet, and I thought probably a wave had splashed me, or maybe some kid had kicked some wet sand on me. But when I looked down—"

"Blerg, that's horrible," Makayla said.

Jules nibbled an apple. "So what did you do?"

"Well, fortunately, I had a towel with me, so I wrapped it around my waist."

"What did Tanner say?" Makayla asked. "Because omigod, Lia, there you were, suddenly *wearing a toga*—"

"I think she probably looked more ancient Egyptian," Abi corrected her. "If Lia only had the towel around her *waist*."

I shrugged. "I'm not sure how it looked. All I told Tanner was that I felt cold, so he gave me his hoodie."

Jules and Makayla went "*Aww.*" And even I thought, *That was really sweet of him.*

Marley twirled the spaghetti on her plate, but she never put any in her mouth. "All right, my turn," she said loudly.

"But Lia's not done yet," Abi protested.

"Yeah, she is," Marley said firmly. She put down her fork.

You want to hear something funny? I knew Marley thought she was rescuing me from A Million Follow-Up Questions, and I appreciated that. But right then I also felt kind of annoyed at her. She'd basically barged into my story just when I was getting to the juicy Tanner part. And even though I had no idea where any of it was going, I could tell my friends were following every word. Because really: Getting your period on a lonely beach up in Maine with a dark-haired boy you'd just kissed whose lips tasted like chili—it was *such* a better My First Period story than Jules's, which was basically about zits and cramps and the second-floor bathroom.

"I choose dare," Marley said. She raised her eyebrows at me, like, *Well?*

I thought.

"Hurry up," Abi said, poking me.

"I'm thinking," I said. Daring Marley was tricky. If I gave her a lame one, like *I dare you to hold your breath for sixty seconds*, it would be like I was saying we should all go easy on her, because she wasn't as cool as the rest of us. Which I definitely didn't think. But if I gave her a hard dare, like showing her bra size, it would be mean to Marley. And I knew she wasn't too happy with the game to begin with.

"Time's up, Lia," Abi declared.

"Wait," I said. "There's a time limit?"

She laughed. "Yeah. Time's up when the rest of us are sick of waiting. So now *we're* going to decide Marley's dare."

"Hey, that's not fair," I protested.

Abi, Jules, and Makayla ignored me. They huddled.

Then Abi smiled at Marley.

"Okay," she said. "Marley, we dare you to give Graydon a love poem. But first we have to read it. And approve it," Abi added.

Makayla nodded. "And you have to sign it."

I swallowed. "Hey, guys. Isn't that a little too—"

"She chose *dare*, Lia," Jules reminded me.

"I know, but . . ." I glanced at Graydon, who was sitting at a lunch table with two other nerdy seventh-grade boys, Jake Lombardi and Ben Maldonado. "That dare affects *other people*."

"Sometimes the game works that way." Abi shrugged. "It's how you play."

The funny thing was, Marley didn't seem to care about the Graydon part.

"I can copy it out of a book, right? I don't have to actually *write* it?" she asked.

Makayla nodded. "You can even print it off your computer, if you want. As long as you sign your name."

The bell rang.

"Oh yeah, and it has to happen by lunchtime tomorrow," Abi announced, laughing for punctuation.

Glad We Spoke

THAT EVENING THE DOORBELL RANG AT EXACTLY six o'clock, and there was Val with her Tuesday Feast. She'd brought us two roast chickens, mashed potatoes, a Greek salad, roasted vegetables, and brownies. She'd also included two pints of vanilla ice cream, so we could à la mode the brownies, if we wanted. Oh, and a jar of fudge, which we could zap in the microwave, to pour on top.

I helped her unpack everything, thanking her like crazy, the way I always did.

She hugged me. "It just makes me happy to help you

all," she said, sighing. "Cooking is the least I can do." Then she added, "Lia, dear, can we chat for a second?"

"Sure," I said.

We sat at the small table in the kitchen. I quickly brushed some cereal crumbs into my lap, hoping she didn't see. Val smiled brightly, but she didn't speak. Was she waiting for something?

"Would you like some tea?" I asked. "Or cider? Or water? I could make lemonade—"

She held up a hand. "No, I'm fine, thanks. Lia, Abi tells me you had a good summer. Lots happened, right?"

It did? I shrugged.

She waited a little. Then she said, "Well, if you ever want to discuss anything . . . if you have any questions—"

"About what?" I asked.

"Oh, anything. Girl stuff. Or *not* girl stuff. Really, anything at all." She seemed to be searching my face for something. "I'm around all the time."

"Oh, I know," I said.

What was going on here, exactly? I had no clue.

And suddenly I got it: *Abi had told her mom the My First Period story. Why would she do a thing like that?*

My cheeks burned. "That's really nice of you, Val, but I'm fine, actually. And also, I talk all the time to my aunt Shelby."

Val's brow puckered. "Right. How *is* Shelby?"

"Great. She has a store and maybe a second one. And omigod, such adorable cats! I always wanted one, but my mom was allergic, so . . ." I was babbling, but I couldn't stop.

Val smiled. "Well, that's all good to hear. I haven't kept up with Shelby, actually. Most of what I remember about her from school was how different she was from your mom."

"What do you mean?" I asked.

"Well, your mom was very serious and very smart. And so sweet. Everybody respected her and loved her so much, you know, sweetheart. I still can't believe—" She hugged me then, so I wouldn't notice she was crying.

My throat ached as I smelled Val's shampoo. Mom had used the same brand. Maybe it was the type they bought at salons: The Official Shampoo of All Moms Everywhere.

Finally Val pulled away. Her face was smiling again. "Anyway, I'm glad we spoke. Anytime you ever want to chat, even if you just feel like hanging out in my kitchen, remember I'm only a few blocks away. Will you promise you'll do that, Lia?"

I wanted to shrivel up like a raisin. Abi's mom was the nicest mom on the planet, and I was lying to her, too, now. Crap. Crap times five hundred.

"I totally promise," I said.

Which—*PING!*—was another lie right there.

❤

The next morning in homeroom, Marley was wearing an Art Institute of Chicago hoodie with pockets in the front. She walked over to Makayla's desk and pulled a folded-up sheet of paper out of one of the pockets.

"Here," she said.

Makayla unfolded the paper, squinting at the strange-looking print. "What *is* this?" she demanded.

"A love poem. It's in Sanskrit. I printed it off the Internet. And see, I signed my name at the bottom."

I started laughing. "That's brilliant, Marley."

"I dunno," Makayla said.

"What don't you know?" I challenged her. "Nobody said it had to be in English!"

"Well, how can we tell it's a love poem?" Makayla argued. "It could be an Indian shopping list, for all we know."

Marley scowled at Makayla. "I'll give you the URL, okay? You can look it up, if you really want. There's an English translation."

"Nah, I believe you," Makayla said. She flicked her hand like she was waving away a housefly. "Go ahead. Just give it to Graydon."

"Right now?"

"Yeah, why not?"

I stood watching with Makayla as Marley walked over to Graydon, who was showing Jake and Ben some card he'd bought for this game they were obsessed with called Phantom.

"Here," Marley said, stuffing the poem into Graydon's hands.

Graydon looked annoyed. "What are you doing?"

"It's a poem. For you."

"Am I supposed to read it?"

"No. It's in Sanskrit."

"Then why are you giving it to me?"

"Marley likes you," Jake sang in Graydon's face.

"Not at all," Marley answered calmly. "You're a perfectly nice person, Graydon, and I think you're incredibly smart. And yes, this is a *love* poem, but I definitely do *not* have a crush on you."

Graydon blushed dark red. "Then don't bother me," he grumbled. He crumpled up the poem and tossed it in the garbage.

Marley turned and walked back to us. "Done," she announced.

All morning, I felt terrible for Graydon. It wasn't Marley's fault that the whole thing was so awkward; really, she didn't have much of a choice about how it went. But I could tell Graydon had been confused, and even worse, embarrassed in front of his friends, which seemed unfair. Truth or Dare was *our* game, and I thought it was wrong to hurt people who weren't even playing, who didn't understand the rules. Plus, Graydon thought Marley was making fun of him, and that was also unfair to Marley.

So before science started I went over to Graydon.

"Can we talk in private?" I asked. "In the hall?"

His eyes narrowed. "Why, Lia? You want to borrow my homework?"

"No," I said. "I mean, if you *want* to share it with me, that would be extremely nice, but it's not *why* I want to talk to you."

He shrugged. I followed him out the door.

"So what's up?" he asked, staring at my knees.

"Um, about that poem Marley gave you," I said. "It wasn't her idea; she didn't *mean* to make fun of you. That wasn't the point."

"There was a point?"

"Well, in a way. It was a sort of prank."

His forehead crumpled. He stuffed his hands in his pockets.

"Not by her," I added. "By other people. Who were playing a game."

"Sounds like fun."

"Yeah," I said, agreeing with his sarcasm. "It really wasn't."

He squinted at me. "And were *you* playing this not-fun game?"

"Me?"

He nodded.

This was not going well. I could feel my face on fire. "Yes, but—"

"Thanks for the explanation, Lia." He pushed the door open and left me standing in the hall.

Bub

AT LUNCH, ABI WAS FURIOUS.

"Mak, who said you and Lia could approve the poem all by yourselves?" she demanded.

Makayla sighed sarcastically. "Sorry we didn't ask for your permission, Abi."

"It's not about permission! This is a game we're playing together. All of us. That includes Jules too."

"I know who's playing," Makayla snapped. "But *you* were the one who said Marley had to complete the dare by lunchtime today, right? So when exactly was she supposed to give the poem to Graydon? They're not even in any of the same classes. So it *had* to be in homeroom, right?"

It always amazed me how Makayla stood up to Abi. Nobody else did, and usually Makayla didn't; but when she did, Abi would get all quaky. Her lips would tremble, her face would flush, and she'd look like she was fighting back tears.

"I can't believe you're saying that," she told Makayla. "Don't you care about our feelings?"

Makayla's shoulders rose. Her voice got louder. "Who said *anything* about not caring? Or about *feelings*? Why are you even bringing that *up*?"

"I don't know, Mak. The way you said all that just now—"

"Look, Abi, just because I don't agree with you and think of something on my *own* doesn't mean I don't care about your feelings. Everything isn't always about *you* and your *feelings*!" Makayla shook her head; her thick ponytail whipped back and forth. "Anyhow, I need to check something about swim practice today. See you guys later." She got up and walked over to the swim team table to sit with her teammates, Sarita and Morgan.

"Well," Jules commented.

I stirred my strawberry yogurt like it needed total concentration. After I ate a couple of spoonfuls, I looked up.

"Can I say something? I think if we're going to keep play-ing Truth or Dare, we should make some definite rules. Like, do we need everybody to witness a dare?"

"I vote yes," Jules said. Abi, whose face still looked rumpled and red, barely nodded.

"Although that's not fair to Marley," I said. "It's not *her* fault that she did the dare in front of just Mak and me."

"Fine," Abi said. She took a shaky breath. "We'll say that Marley's dare counted. But from now on everybody in the game has to witness every dare. Although maybe Mak doesn't even want to play."

"What makes you say that?" Marley asked.

"I mean, *look* at her," Abi grumbled. "She seems per-fectly happy with her other friends."

We all looked at Mak, who was laughing loudly with Sarita.

"Can we agree on one other thing?" I said quickly, before the conversation turned into Let's All Talk Behind Makayla's Back. "Can we have a rule that everything we say in the game—all the truths—are private? And we don't tell anybody else?"

Marley bit the crust off her grilled cheese sandwich. "Who would we tell?"

"I don't know," I said, pretending to think. "Like maybe someone's parent?"

"Are you saying somebody *told* somebody?" Abi's eyes flashed at me. By then she was looking like normal Abi, leader Abi.

I swallowed some more yogurt. "I just think we need a rule. From now on."

"Okay with me," Marley said.

"Whatever," Abi said, crumpling her napkin. "You know what, Lia? I don't even want to talk about this game anymore. I don't care if we never even play it again."

The funny thing was, by dismissal Abi and Mak were best friends again. Maybe they'd talked it over during sixth-period art, or during Spanish, which they had together at the end of the day. All I knew for sure was that they'd come up with a joke they both found hilarious—calling people "bub."

Like when Mak and Abi saw Graydon get on the bus, they called out, "Bye, bub! See you tomorrow, bub!" and practically fell over, laughing. And when Mr. Halloran walked past us to get his car, Abi shouted, "Have a nice afternoon!" When he waved back, she and Mak muttered, "Bub," and went into hysterics.

"What's so funny about the word 'bub'?" Marley asked me.

I shrugged. "No clue. But it's better than 'dahling.' And at least they're not fighting."

The five of us walked a few short blocks to the Maplebrook Diner, the way we sometimes did after school. We had about an hour, because Marley had a tutor coming to her house, Jules had to go to the dentist, and Mak had a swim practice at the YMCA pool. But there was enough time for us to order our usual—milk shakes for everybody except Abi, who always had two scoops of cookie dough ice cream with butterscotch syrup, whipped cream, and gummy teddy bears on top.

I couldn't help wondering if we'd play Truth or Dare. Not that I wanted to; after the Graydon incident, the whole game had kind of soured for me, really. But—here's the weird thing—a teeny part of me felt disappointed *not* to play. I think I missed telling my made-up story, watching my friends hang on every detail. I missed the surprise in their faces: *"Lia? All that happened to nice little you?"*

The waitress brought us our orders. Her name was Maggie, and she hated us, maybe because we always made too much noise and one time forgot to leave a tip. We waited for her to walk away from our table, and then Abi stuck out her tongue behind Maggie's back.

"Great look, bub," Mak told Abi, laughing. "I think you should do a selfie like that and send it to Nick."

"Shut up, bub," Abi said. "*You* send him a selfie."

Marley caught my eye. *Bub*, she mouthed.

"No, I'm serious," Mak insisted. She took a giant sip of her mint chocolate chip shake. "Hey, bub, I have a question: If Nick asked you out, would you go?"

Abi snorted. "Are you insane, Mak? He's, like, fifteen. My mom would have a heart attack."

"So the answer is no?"

"It's a stupid question," Marley declared. "Because there's no way a fifteen-year-old boy would ask out a twelve-year-old girl. If he did, he'd be a creepy loser, so why would you *want* to go out with him, anyway?"

Everyone stared at Marley.

"Well, Lia went out with Tanner this summer," Mak argued. She cocked her head at me. "And didn't you say he was in high school?"

"Well, going *into* high school," I said. "As a freshman. But we didn't *go out.*"

"You didn't?" Jules asked. "It sounded like you did."

"No, we just walked on the beach together. A few times."

"And kissed," Jules reminded me.

"Yeah, well." I shrugged. "Then I found out he had this other girlfriend. Named Logan. So I dumped him."

"He was seeing you behind Logan's back?" Jules looked outraged.

"Sort of. Although truthfully, she was pretty nasty, so . . ."

"Even if she was," Jules said. "Cheating is just wrong. Tanner totally deserved to be dumped."

I slurped some chocolate milk shake. "I know, right?"

"Was he really upset?" Mak asked me. "When you dumped him?"

"Well, he was confused. I didn't tell him I knew about Logan."

"Why not?" Jules asked. "If it was me, I would've made sure he knew *exactly* why. Anyway, the truth is always bound to come out, right?"

She said it like it was a thing she'd read somewhere.

I was suddenly aware of Abi's eyes glaring at me. Maybe she didn't like it that we were talking about my fake boy-friend instead of hers.

I sipped my chocolate shake and rolled the corner of my napkin.

"Speaking of truth," Abi said slowly. "Can we talk about something, Lia?"

"Sure," I said.

"I don't know how to say this," Abi said, glancing at Jules and Mak. "But we're all best friends, right? So we're supposed to trust each other and be honest with each other. Not just when we're playing a game."

My heart thudded. Was she about to expose all my lies? "Yeah, of course," I said quickly.

"And lately I've been thinking about this a *lot*, Lia: You know, you've never talked to us about when your mom died. I don't mean about the accident—I mean, how it felt. To you."

Something passed over me then, like a shiver. I couldn't speak; I could feel my heart banging against my chest.

"What?" Marley snapped. "Are you *joking*, Abi?"

"No, Marley. I'm really not."

"But that's an awful thing to make Lia talk about!"

"Why?" Abi asked. "We're her *best friends*, right? If she can't talk about it with us, who can she talk to?"

"Yeah, I know, but—"

Abi ignored Marley. "We're only asking because we care about you, Lia. And you never even mention it, you know?"

Nobody spoke. They were all looking at me, including Marley, who was shaking her head like, *Don't do it.*

I could have refused. Really, I wanted to refuse. Even now, the Accident hurt my stomach to talk about, and I didn't trust myself not to cry.

But I knew Abi was testing me. If I refused to answer, I would fail. In front of everyone. All of my friends.

Besides, how could you pick some truths to share and keep others to yourself? What were the rules for that? Maybe there weren't any.

"It's okay," I said to Marley. "I don't mind."

She shrugged.

So then I told my friends about the minutes and days after the Accident, how I kept wondering about the stupid guy's stupid phone conversation and how he and his wife showed up at our house with the waxy cookies.

Also how Dad pitied him, but Nate and I thought he was a monster.

How after he left, I threw away my phone.

How we felt grateful and shocked and embarrassed by all the food people kept bringing us.

But mostly how sad we felt about Mom. And still did.

Jules put her arm around my shoulder. "Poor Lia," she said. Her eyelashes were wet.

"Can I tell you guys another truth?" I said. "I hate the 'Poor Lia' stuff. I'm really okay."

"We know you are," Mak said. "But thanks for telling us all that."

She got up from the table to hug me, and so did Abi. Once again I felt like limp lettuce inside a sandwich. But also—and this surprised me—glad I finally told those things to my friends.

Even though Marley didn't say a word to me and left the diner without finishing her milk shake.

Fascinating New Developments

WHEN I CAME HOME FROM THE DINER, NATE WAS sitting in the kitchen eating Val's brownies drowned in hot fudge.

"Want some?" he asked.

I shook my head.

He made a noise through his nose. "Don't tell me you're on a diet."

"Of course not."

"Good. It's so stupid when skinny girls diet. So how are your friends?"

"My *friends?* Why are you even asking?"

"How's Jules?" He grinned. His teeth were smeared with chocolate.

I narrowed my eyes at my brother. "She's fine. And even if she wasn't, it's none of your business, Fungus Face."

"Whatever. Oh yeah, speaking of fungus. Guess who's coming this weekend. Aunt Shelby."

I froze. "She is? How do you know?"

"She called Dad, and he called me. She would have called *you* if you had a phone."

When I didn't respond, Nate said, "So what happened between you two, anyway? Did you, like, fight with her this summer?"

"Why? What makes you ask that?"

"I dunno. A weird vibe you've been giving off since you got back from Maine."

"I'm not giving off any *weird vibes.*"

"If you say so, Fungus Breath." He licked some fudge off his fingers. "But if you *did* fight with her, I wouldn't blame you. To be honest, I couldn't believe you lasted there as long as you did."

Neither could I, the more I thought about it. I went upstairs and threw my backpack on my bed. Why was Aunt Shelby showing up *now*? Abi said she'd ask her mom if we could have a sleepover Saturday night, but if Aunt

Shelby was here for the weekend, Dad would probably say I couldn't go. Plus, there was the whole awkwardness of seeing my aunt again. Dad had instructed me to write her a thank-you note for the summer, and I knew it was the polite thing to do, but every time I sat down to write it, my brain clogged like a hairy sink. *Dear Aunt Shelby, I really appreciated how you spied on me. Thanks for humiliating me by inviting Tanner. I'm so grateful for the bras, which I've buried somewhere in my closet.*

The truth was, I still hadn't forgiven Aunt Shelby. I didn't want her to visit. I had nothing to say to her.

Val was right: My aunt *was* so different from my mom.

And that's who I missed. Who I really *wanted* to see.

I reached under my bed for a bin. I didn't even care which one—seashells, sea glass, marbles, dice, charms, erasers, buttons, pebbles. Any of my collections would soothe me for a few minutes as I sifted through the pieces, held them up to the light, maybe even arranged them in a different way as I put them back in the bin.

This time I picked buttons. And as I sorted them, I thought, Wouldn't it be wonderful if all the best memories—of Mom, for example—were a collection? And you could reach under your bed and hold them in your hands whenever you wanted? Whenever you needed them?

And when you held them up to the light, they wouldn't disappear?

That night I couldn't sleep. My brain just wouldn't turn off: I worried about Aunt Shelby showing up and doing something that made me even madder. Or meeting my friends and saying something disastrous (*Lia told you she kissed Tanner? Not according to my spy!*) I worried about my friends hanging out without me. I also worried about Marley—why had she left the diner so weirdly yesterday? Not even saying anything after I'd talked about the Accident—was she mad at me for some reason? I couldn't understand what I'd done to *her*. And if everyone was hanging out at Abi's this weekend, would Marley go there without me? That didn't seem like the best idea, but I couldn't exactly advise her not to go on her own.

The next morning, by the time I got to homeroom, Marley was already there. She was wearing a blue Field Museum Chicago sweatshirt that was so big it must have been meant for a unisex giant, and she was drawing in her sketchpad. She didn't notice me—or anyway, that's what she pretended.

I tapped her shoulder. "Hey, Marley."

She just kept drawing. It looked like a knotty tree with swirly branches that went on forever. A fantasy tree.

"I love your tree," I said. "You're such a good artist."

"Thanks."

She didn't look up. So I just took the seat next to her.

"Hi, Lia," Ruby Lewis said, as she flopped into the seat in front of me.

"Hi," I replied. Ruby was nice enough, but she was the opposite of me in terms of development, and it was weird how she never wore a bra. In fact, a bunch of boys in our class called her Booby Ruby and other names that were even worse. Didn't she hear them? Didn't she care?

Maybe she could borrow one of Marley's sweatshirts, I thought. Because Marley had a million of them, one for everywhere she'd gone in Chicago, it seemed.

I turned to my right, where Marley was sitting. But she wasn't there.

When I wasn't paying attention again, she'd slipped away.

At lunch Marley didn't sit at our table. And as soon as Mak sat down, she told Abi that she'd "just remembered" about a "swim team thing" she had to go to that weekend, which meant she couldn't do the sleepover. That was when I mentioned that Aunt Shelby was supposed to visit on Saturday, so probably I couldn't come, either.

Abi's eyes filled with angry tears. "Fine," she snapped. "Then it'll just be Jules and me!"

What about Marley? I almost asked. But for Marley's sake, I decided not to.

We didn't talk very much that day; we were all a bit grumpy, I guess, and after school Marley was staying late for tutoring, while Mak had band rehearsal. At dismissal I saw Val drive by to pick up Abi and Jules. They didn't tell me where they were going, and I didn't ask.

I was just about to start walking home by myself when Val's car pulled up.

She rolled down the window and smiled at me. I could hear a twangy, ballady song on the radio and feel the cold gush of air-conditioning.

"Want a lift home?" Val asked sweetly.

I should have said no. If Abi had wanted me in her car, she would have invited me herself. I knew she was mad about me bailing on the sleepover—I was sure she'd taken it as an attack on her feelings. And frankly, by now I was getting pretty sick of Abi's feelings, the way they shoved everybody else out of the room.

But there was something so inviting about getting into

a mom-mobile after a weird day at school. Val was always so comforting. I was tired and sweaty. And I was about to have a crap weekend with my aunt, which made me feel sorry for myself.

So I got in.

Jules smiled at me, but Abi barely even looked in my direction. She was just going on and on to Val about her Spanish test, how unfair it was, focusing on a chapter the teacher hadn't even covered yet. Then she started telling her mom about Natalie Palmeiro, who got sent to the assistant principal's office for cheating off Graydon's math test and was crying so hard she had to stay with Mrs. Garcia, the school nurse, for the rest of the day. The whole time Abi was describing all this, Jules was nodding and making little agreement sounds and Val was asking questions like, "Did anyone say anything?" and "Then what happened?"

I asked myself, *If Mom were around, would I tell her the same meaningless gossip? And when we were in private, would I talk about my friends, and the Truth or Dare game, and maybe Aunt Shelby, and ask her questions about my Lack of Development?*

Would she answer like Val, if I did?

Or tell me something I don't already know?

"Here you are, Lia, safe and sound," Val announced in a cheery voice as she pulled into my driveway. A look crossed her face; I guessed she thought she probably shouldn't have said "safe and sound," even as a joke.

"Thanks for the ride," I called, waving at my friends as I got out.

"See you Monday," Abi said. She didn't smile or wave back. "Have fun with your *aunt*."

The way she said it, it was like "your so-called aunt." Like she thought I was using Aunt Shelby as a made-up excuse. Or no: as a lie.

By the time I got up for breakfast on Saturday morning, Aunt Shelby was already sitting in the kitchen with Dad. Right away she jumped up to hug me. "Niecelet!" she cried.

I watched Dad's face over her shoulder as we hugged. He looked tense and uncomfortable, I thought, as he chewed his English muffin. Maybe Aunt Shelby had been criticizing his job again.

"So how are things?" Aunt Shelby asked as she studied my pajamas. "Any fascinating new developments?"

Seriously? Had she actually just used that word— DEVELOPMENTS?

"Nope," I muttered. I crossed my arms over my chest. "How are the cats?"

"Oh, they're fine, except now Escobar needs dental surgery. Can you believe that? The vet says it'll cost a fortune."

Dad harrumphed. "Well, talk to me if any of them need reading glasses." He poured some sugar into his coffee. "Lee-lee, your aunt was thinking of taking you shopping today."

"Oh, you don't have to," I told her quickly.

She grinned. "Sure I do! That's what aunts are for! Now you go get your breakfast and do your homework or whatever, while I finish up here with your dad."

I glanced at Dad again, but he just drank his coffee, refusing to give away hints about what needed "finishing up" between them. So I grabbed a bowl of cereal, brought it upstairs to my room, and read Book Three of Hiber-Nation until it was time to get dressed.

Whatever Works

AN HOUR LATER AUNT SHELBY AND I WERE strolling through Maplebrook Mall, eating banana walnut froyo (her) and a double scoop of chocolate peanut butter ice cream (me). Dessert before lunch—it was kind of crazy, but I wasn't about to argue when Aunt Shelby offered to buy me a cone. I'd even started thinking that maybe this mall trip wouldn't be too horrific, when she suddenly said, "So, Lia. I see you're not wearing any of the bras we bought in Maine, including the new ones I sent home with you."

I froze. It was that obvious?

"You're dripping, buttercup." She pointed to my ice cream cone. "Why not? They didn't fit?"

"It wasn't a question of them fitting."

"No? What was it, then?"

Blerg. We were going to have this conversation; I didn't see any escape route.

I asked if we could sit. We found an empty bench in front of Candie's Candles, a store that smelled like fake cinnamon. When the fake-cinnamon-candle-smell mixed with the taste of my chocolate peanut butter ice cream, I suddenly felt mall-sick. I tossed my drippy cone in a nearby trash can.

"So?" Aunt Shelby said.

Part of me just wanted to get up and zoom out of the mall, but I also knew that if I didn't speak up, I'd never forgive myself. Because it wasn't as if I didn't think things, or feel things, about the way my aunt had acted this summer. Besides, she always said how she wanted "special time" for "girl talk." Well, so we should finally have it, right?

I took a deep breath of cinnamon mall-air. "The problem is that I didn't want *any* bras in the first place. You *made* me buy them. Then you stuffed them into my bag, along with these other ones I didn't even choose. That had *padding*. Which, truthfully, I don't understand."

"You don't understand what? How to wear them? I could show you—"

"No," I said. "What I don't understand was why you'd give me something so *fake.* Especially after telling me there was nothing wrong with being a late bloomer, how Mom was one, and you—"

"It's true. We were."

"So then if it's that just the way we *are,* why would you give me bras that say it's *not* okay? That I should basically *fake* having boobs?"

She blinked. "You mean the padding?"

I nodded.

"Oh boy. Oh boy. Lia, I'm so, so sorry." My aunt grabbed my ice-cream-sticky hands. "That's *not* what I was thinking *at all.* You're beautiful; I'd never, ever suggest that you weren't! I only gave you those extra bras because I thought *you* cared."

"Why would you think that?"

"Oh, a lot of reasons. How you wouldn't model any bras for Winnie and me. The way you never wore bathing suits to the beach. How you freaked when I asked you about it. How you snapped at me when I suggested suit shopping—"

I watched a mom drag her wriggling little kid into the

Gap. "Well, yeah. I did feel kind of self-conscious on the beach. I mean, compared to Tanner's girlfriend in her stupid bikini. And I definitely wish something was happening with my body by *now*. But I'd never *lie* about how I look."

"That's good to hear," Aunt Shelby said. "It makes me proud of you! I'd just been worrying that maybe—" She left her sentence stranded.

"Maybe what?"

Aunt Shelby sighed. "Well, back in Maine you mentioned Val. And her daughter."

"Abi. What about them?"

Aunt Shelby ate her last bite of froyo. She put her empty cup on the bench. "You really wanna hear, Lia?"

I didn't know if I did. Maybe I didn't. But I nodded.

"Okay. You remember that Val and I went to school together, right? So. When we were in seventh grade, Val used to torment me in gym. In the locker room. She called me names like Pancake, Tortilla, Ironing Board—"

"Wait. Really? Why?"

"Well, for one thing, I was sort of your standard weird kid, I guess. My voice was too loud, I dressed funny, I constantly challenged people, all that stuff. Everyone thought your mom was Miss Wonderful, and I was like her mutant little sister who didn't fit in. Maplebrook was *not* a good environment for me."

I nodded, even though I'd never thought about my aunt as a middle schooler before.

"Plus, in seventh grade I was almost completely boob-less," Aunt Shelby continued. "Flatter than you, Lia, if you can believe it. And Val got all her friends to join in the teasing. One time they stuffed a baby-size undershirt in my locker. I accused Val, and she just laughed. The next day there was a diaper. After that a onesie. This went on for a while. I didn't know what to do."

"That's horrible!" I said. "Did you tell Grandma?"

She shook her head. "Your grandmother was always too freaked by body stuff. It was a generation thing, I guess. Anyway, I finally I told my big, strong sister—your mom. We fought a lot as kids—as grown-ups, too, you know—but I knew she'd always be there for me."

Aunt Shelby paused a few seconds, took a few breaths, then continued. "Jessie wanted to confront Val herself, but I begged her not to, because I was convinced it would just make things worse. So then Jessie took me shopping for bras with just the slightest bit of padding. Not to lie about myself, you understand—just to stop the bullying."

That shocked me. Mom would never have worn boob enhancers herself. I didn't even have to look through her underwear drawer to know this. "And it worked?"

"Actually, it did. Val and her friends moved on to another

target, a girl who obviously hadn't gotten her period yet, because she was flat." Aunt Shelby leaned toward me and combed her fingers through my hair. "Sometimes I wished I'd stood up for myself another way, you know? With brilliant words, or a hilarious joke. A magic potion, maybe. For a while I had this fantasy I'd march up to Val in front of her friends and shout something like, 'Yes, I'm flat, okay? Deal with it!' But the truth is, I couldn't have pulled that off when I was twelve. And when someone's picking on you, you do whatever works, I guess."

My brain had emptied; I couldn't speak. Val, the sweetest, nicest mom in Maplebrook, who drove me in her mom-mobile and brought feasts to our house every Tuesday and hugged Abi's friends all the time and let us eat chocolate cupcakes in Abi's room—she'd bullied Aunt Shelby in middle school? She'd made my aunt wear bras in self-defense?

And then picked on another girl for the same stuff? I didn't think Aunt Shelby was lying. Why should she? But still, how was this even possible?

Not to mention the part about Mom buying her little sister padding. Which went against everything I knew about my sports-bra-wearing, hardly-any-makeup-wearing mother.

Then something occurred to me. "Did you think someone was bullying *me?*" I asked my aunt. "Is that why you bought me those padded bras?"

"Listen, Lia, I have no experience with daughter stuff, you know? So I mess up sometimes, like I did with Yazmin. But I only hired her because I care about you. I worry about you. And I'm not around very much; I don't have access to facts. All I have is my intuition." She patted her chest, as if that's where she stored her intuition.

"And your intuition told you I was being bullied?" I pressed.

"Yeah, actually." She studied my face. "*Are* you?"

"No, I'm not," I answered firmly. "The only girl I know who gets teased is Ruby Lewis, and it's for the opposite reason. And it's by the boys, not the girls. Besides, if anyone tried to bully *me*, my friends would protect me."

Aunt Shelby patted my knee. "Then I shouldn't have worried, niecelet. Sorry I even brought it up."

Rubber Band

ON THE RIDE HOME FROM THE MALL, AUNT Shelby talked mostly about Herb 'n' Legend, the new store she wanted to open. She said she had the perfect space picked out two towns over, near Winnie's Intimates, but she still needed an investor. Unfortunately, Dad told her this morning that he wasn't interested, but maybe she could still convince him—

My aunt went on and on about her new store, but I stopped listening. Something about what she'd said in the mall had begun to trouble me: How Val could just *tell* the other girl hadn't gotten her period.

Because that girl was boobless.

And the rule was: *If boobless, then no period.*

Like Marley.

And like me.

Even though I'd told my friends the My First Period story.

This meant: My friends knew it wasn't true. OR

They suspected it wasn't true. OR

They'd figure out that it wasn't true.

And if they didn't figure it out on their own, Val might even tell them.

Also I thought this: According to Aunt Shelby, Val used to be a Mean Girl. Now Val was officially the nicest mom in Maplebrook. Do mean girls outgrow their meanness when they grow up? Or, underneath the sweet, cupcake-baking outside, maybe Val was still capable of meanness. Maybe she was even teaching Abi how to be mean.

Not that Abi needed a whole bunch of lessons. Really, she was already plenty mean enough.

I started chewing my thumbnail, even though my thumb skin was turning red. Any way I looked at it, I knew I was in trouble. And it seemed as if I had only two options.

Option one: Admit to my friends that I'd lied to

them—about getting my period, my first kiss, the whole dumping Tanner business. But then my friends might not still be my friends. Especially after Abi's speech in the diner about best friends trusting one another and telling the truth.

Option Two: Stop being boobless. This would entail wearing padded bras to school and lying about myself, but it would also mean not blowing the My First Period story. Or the My First Kiss story. Or the Tanner saga. And therefore not being exposed as a liar and therefore also keeping my friends. Who I needed ridiculously.

Although I really, really did *not* want to wear a stupid padded bra. To school or anywhere else.

It was so unfair how my whole life was suddenly Pads and Padding!

But then I remembered what Aunt Shelby said about solving her own problem: *You do whatever works.* And the fact that her big sister—my mom—had bought those padded bras for her: Well, it almost seemed, in a funny way, as if she'd bought them for me, too.

On Monday I felt as if I had a giant rubber band around my chest and that if I breathed too deeply, or coughed, it would snap. The funny thing was, the bra barely made me look any different. I mean, yes, the cups had padding, but under my sweater, the padding barely showed. I'd been terrified that I'd walk around the corridors looking as if I'd stuffed a couple of socks in my undershirt and anytime someone bumped into me, you'd hear *psssssss*, like the sound our sofa pillows make when you accidentally sit on them. But no. The cups were okay. They didn't deflate or make weird noises. The problem was the *entire bra*, how it made me feel as if I had a neon sign flashing on my chest: *Yes, people of Earth, I am wearing a padded bra. Move along. Nothing to see here, folks.*

Although wait: You're allowed to look just long enough to prove that I'm no longer boobless. Then you should move along. Thank you. Signed, The Management.

In homeroom Mak didn't comment about my appearance, and Marley just spent the whole time sketching. And when Abi came running into our room she didn't stop to focus on my chest.

Instead she handed chocolate lollipops to Mak, Marley, and me. Around the stick of each lollipop was a red ribbon and a tiny note that said SORRY ☺

"What's this for?" Mak asked. She sounded a little suspicious, I thought.

Abi smiled sweetly. "Well, I was a little bit evil on Friday, wasn't I? But over the weekend I got my period, so PMS mood swing, I guess. You forgive me?"

"Of course," I answered.

"So I'll see you guys at lunch?"

"Sure," said Mak, shrugging like she didn't care one way or the other.

I glanced at Marley. She didn't answer Abi or smile or even look interested in the chocolate lollipop, which she stuffed into the front pocket of her Chicago Bulls hoodie. I tried to read her face, but I couldn't see her eyes behind her glasses. And when the end-of-homeroom bell rang, I knew I wouldn't see her again until lunch. I thought of running after her and asking, *Are you still mad at me, for some reason?* Or possibly: *Are you having symptoms, and is that why you're acting so weird, all of a sudden?* But I had the feeling she wouldn't answer—or that if she did, maybe I wouldn't want to hear it.

Third period was PE. As soon as I got to the locker room, I realized that I hadn't thought through this part of the day. Obviously, I had to take off my sweater—but I wasn't ready to show off Aunt Shelby's bra. This one was okay-enough looking: It didn't have a rhinestone or "My First Padded Bra" embroidered into it, and it was a completely decent shade of pink. But I knew that once my sweater was off, you'd be able to tell the cups were padded. And suddenly the thought of everyone seeing how I'd basically strapped *tiny pillows* to my chest made me feel like barfing.

So what I did was undress in the bathroom, then sprint into the locker room changing area like, *Yay me, here I am, totally stoked for volleyball!* When PE was over, I sprinted back into the bathroom like I desperately needed to pee and came out of the stall two minutes later, dressed for fourth-period English.

As I stepped out of the bathroom, Abi, Jules, and Mak were waiting for me.

"Lia, you all right?" Abi asked.

"What do you mean?" I said.

"Why are you avoiding us?" Mak asked. "We suddenly have cooties, or something?"

I stared at my shoes. "I just . . . have this . . . sort of rash. On my chest."

"Oh, gross. Is it itchy?" Jules scratched her elbow. Probably she was remembering her poison ivy.

"Incredibly. But I'm sure it's not contagious."

Abi frowned. "But how do you know that, Lia? Did you go to the doctor?"

"Actually, my aunt Shelby knows a lot about skin things. So this weekend? When she visited? She brought me this lotion from some plant in the rain forest. I don't remember the name, but it's really kind of stinky, so . . ." I made a wincing sort of face.

"You could borrow some baby powder," Jules offered. "I keep some in my locker."

"That's really nice," I told her. "But no thanks! Because I don't think I should mix baby powder and this Amazon lotion thingy. My chest might explode, haha."

Abi put her arm around me. "Listen, Lia," she said softly as she nudged me a few steps away from Mak and Jules. "If you need to go to the doctor and you don't want your dad to go . . . I mean, my mom would totally take you whenever."

"Thanks, Abi," I said.

"So if you still have this rash tomorrow morning, just tell me, okay? And my mom will make an appointment at our dermatologist. He's really nice."

Up close to Abi I could see she had a bunch of black-heads on her nose, like poppy seeds. Maybe she went to the nice dermatologist to pop them. Or whatever derma-tologists did. I didn't like to think about it, to be perfectly honest.

"That's really nice of your mom," I said. "And you."

"It's not a big deal. We're totally here for you, Lia. We all are."

"Thanks, Abi. I know."

All of a sudden hot, messy tears sprang into my eyes. Not only because Abi had reminded me about my mom, or rather, my lack of a mom, but also because I felt guilty about lying to my friends. Why had I made up a story about some nonexistent rash? Who cared if my dumb bra had a teeny bit of padding? For all I knew, my friends wore padding too. And the fact that I hadn't even *noticed* if they wore padding just proved how silly it was to lie about it.

And here was Abi being so sweet to me, offering her own mom like a substitute for my missing one. My friends were awesome; I was crazy to think that Abi was just mean, or that Val was just an older Mean Girl with a mom-ponytail. What was wrong with me? Maybe my brain was scrambled due to hormones.

If I even had any. Probably I didn't; that would explain my need for a fake-boob bra.

I scratched my pretend rash on my pretend chest.

"Thank you," I repeated, to no one in particular.

Body Switch

AT LUNCH ABI HAD "A FUN QUESTION" FOR US: "If you could switch bodies with anyone else you know personally, whose body would it be?"

Mak groaned. "Is this Truth or Dare? Because you know I'm not playing that game anymore."

"It's just a *question*," Abi replied. "But everyone should still answer truthfully."

"Can I say a movie star?" Jules asked, giggling. That day she was wearing a pair of complicated dangly earrings her sister had passed on to her, and when she laughed, all the earring parts quivered.

"Not unless you know the movie star personally," Abi replied.

"Okay," Jules said. "Then it would have to be Mak."

Mak snorted. "No, seriously, Julesie."

"I *am* serious. You're so strong. You have arm muscles. You're tall. You don't sunburn, and you look like a swimmer goddess in a bathing suit."

"Oh, pul-lease," Makayla said. But she was trying not to smile. "Who would you pick, Abi?"

"Jules," Abi said. She was looking right at Mak, though, as if she were challenging her.

Jules rolled her eyes.

"No, it's true," Abi told Jules. "You're so small and curvy. You look cute in everything, even when you're wearing one of your sister's old hand-me-downs."

"Well, thanks." Jules smiled and blushed pink, as if she didn't even hear the part about "old hand-me-downs." "What about you, Mak?"

Mak chewed her turkey sandwich thoughtfully. Then she answered, "Well, Sarita, I guess. She has really long arms and legs, which is a big advantage if you're a swimmer. And her feet are really big too, so she gets a lot of flipper action."

Abi guffawed.

"Why is that funny?" Mak demanded.

"I don't know. I didn't expect you'd say, 'I'd rather be Bigfoot.'"

"Because you're not a swimmer. And maybe you're slightly jealous of Sarita."

"What? Why would I be?"

"I don't know, Abi. You tell me."

Abi and Mak glared at each other across the lunch table. Abi's lower lip started to tremble. Mak hunched her shoulders, like she was expecting an attack.

Uh-oh, I thought. *Here we go.*

Jules must have been thinking the same thing, because she turned to me. "What about you, Lia?" she asked loudly.

"Let's all guess," Abi said. "Ooh, I know. Ruby Lewis?"

"Shut up," Jules said, giggling.

"Seriously. What is Ruby's *problem*? Someone needs to talk to that girl."

"And say what?" Mak challenged Abi. "'Excuse me, but have you considered not jiggling quite so much?'"

Jules smiled sympathetically. "Ruby just needs a bra. Someone should tell her."

"Like who?" Mak demanded.

"Doesn't she have a mom?" I asked.

"Divorced. Ruby lives with her dad," Abi informed

us. "What I heard was she sees her mom, like, once a year. Tops."

"Don't say 'tops,'" Mak said.

Jules put her hand over her mouth to cover up her giggle. "But really, only once a year? That's so *sad*."

Then she peeked at me guiltily, as if Ruby's once-a-year mom situation wasn't the worst thing she could think of. I pretended not to notice.

"You know what I think?" Abi said. "Someone should go to the mall and buy Ruby a bra and just, like, slip it into her gym locker."

"What? *No*," I said, horrified.

Everyone looked at me curiously. Even Marley, who hadn't said a word the whole time.

"Why not?" Abi pressed. "It would be an anonymous gift."

"I just don't think she'd take it the right way," I said quickly. "What if someone's mom talked to Ruby instead? Like Val, maybe?" I turned to Abi. "Because, I mean, if anyone's mom could do something like that, it would be yours."

As I said this I got the irony of suggesting Val, of all people, to talk to Ruby instead of slipping a bra into Ruby's locker. But even so, I meant it as a compliment to Val.

So I was surprised that Abi scowled at me. "My mom

has enough stuff to do these days, you know? And anyway, Lia, you never gave your answer."

"About the body-switching thing?" I took a breath. "Well, I hate to admit this, but I'd have to say Logan."

"You mean that girl Tanner cheated on?" Jules asked. Her eyes widened.

I nodded. "Yeah. She wasn't a nice person, or anything, but truthfully, I wish I could look like her in a bikini."

Was Jules finally noticing my fake chest? She was definitely looking me over. "Well, Lia, I'm sure you'd look fine in a bikini, if you ever wore one. And don't forget, Tanner cheated on Logan to be with *you*."

"Yeah," I said. "I guess."

Also, was Abi narrowing her eyes as if she didn't believe me? Or was it just my guilty conscience?

"Lia, how old did you say Logan was?" Abi asked.

Had I said anything about Logan's age? I couldn't remember, but I didn't want to contradict myself. "Fourteen, maybe?"

Abi blinked. "Wow. So you're saying that this Tanner guy cheated on a gorgeous girl his own age to make out with *you*."

"We didn't make out. We kissed. Once." I was sweating; soon I'd need to wring out the padding.

"Maybe he thought Lia was nicer than Logan," Jules suggested.

"Mmmf," Abi said. "Maybe." She was having an eye conversation with Mak; I was sure of it.

"What about you, Marley?" I asked desperately.

Marley picked a blob of cheese off her pizza. "What about me *what*?"

"Who would you pick?"

"Whose nose would I pick?"

"No, you dummy," Mak said. "Whose body?"

"Yeah, I heard the question, Makayla. *Well.* Since you're forcing me to join in this conversation, I have to tell you truthfully that I think it's a stupid question and I refuse to answer it. I think we should all be happy with the bodies we have and not be jealous of other people. And not be making fun of Ruby, who's actually a very nice person. Also, I think worrying about how you look in a bikini is boring and a waste of brainpower. If you really want to wear a bikini, Lia, then just *do* it."

I felt slapped.

Abi's mouth twisted. "Marley, can you please explain something? Why do you always have to ruin everything?"

"I'm not ruining anything," Marley said calmly. "You said I had to answer your question, so I did."

"It's Marley's opinion," I said weakly.

Abi ignored me. "And, Marley, why are you even sitting with us if you don't want to join in? Go sit with your boyfriend, Graydon. You know you want to!"

Marley shot me a look from under her bangs.

"Why don't you kiss him, Marley?" Abi continued. "Go ahead. We all dare you."

"Not me," I muttered.

Abi raised her eyebrows. "Really, Lia? Why? Oh, because *you* like him too?"

"Nobody likes anybody," Marley growled. She stood. "You know what? I'm done. I really *don't* understand why you all keep playing stupid games or answering Abi's stupid questions. Any of you. Especially Lia."

She grabbed her remaining pizza crust, tossed it into the nearby trash, and headed quickly toward the lunchroom doors.

"Marley, wait," I said.

But the thing was, she never did.

Closed Fist

I DIDN'T SEE MARLEY UNTIL DISMISSAL, AND ONLY then because I stalked her. Well, not *stalked* her, but waited by her locker, where I knew she couldn't avoid me. And then followed her out of the building as she tried to escape.

"Marley, are you going to keep ignoring me?" I shouted at her back.

A block from school she slowed down to let me catch up. "I'm not ignoring you, Lia. I just have nothing else to say."

"Marley," I said, trying to catch my breath. "I know you never liked the Truth or Dare game; you said so at the beginning. But it's over; we're not even playing it anymore!"

"Yeah, and now everyone's being all *truthful* with each other, right?" Her eyes pierced me through her glasses.

"Well, yeah," I said.

She kicked some pebbles. "Lia, I used to feel like we got each other, you know? But lately I don't know. I don't know *you*."

"What do you mean?"

"The way you let Abi bully you into talking about your mom—"

"She didn't bully me. I told you, I *wanted* to talk about it!"

"Yeah? So how come you never did before that time in the diner? Plus, the way you made up that ridiculous story about kissing Tanner."

"Why was it ridiculous?"

"High school freshmen don't make out with twelve-year-olds. If he'd kissed you on a public beach, someone would have punched him or told your aunt. And all that stuff about his nasty girlfriend with the bikini body—"

"But Logan *does* look great in a bikini! That was true!"

"Okay, whatever. Fine. And the way you lied about your period."

We stared at each other.

"What?" I could barely breathe.

"That was a lie, wasn't it? You haven't started your period yet, have you?"

"No," I murmured. "You're right. I haven't." My arms crossed my padded chest. "How could you tell?"

"I'm a visual person, right? I notice things." She pushed her bangs out of her eyes. "Like how whenever Jules gets her period, her hair is flat and greasy and she has zits on her forehead. And when Makayla got her first period? I knew it was coming, because she kept rubbing her belly like she had cramps."

"What about Abi?"

"Truthfully, I haven't noticed much, except how moody and mean she's been lately."

I nodded. It was a relief to hear someone say it. "And me?"

"You? Okay, you, Lia." She began counting off her fingers. "You've been totally flat until today. Your hair is always the same. Your skin isn't oily. You don't get zits. You don't smell after gym. You don't talk about food cravings. You never act tired or crampy or grumpy for no reason. Should I go on?"

I shook my head. I couldn't bear to hear any more symptoms.

"So how come you lied about it?" Marley asked.

"I don't know," I wailed. "All that camp talk, I guess; I just felt so left out. Didn't you?"

Marley stuffed her hands into the front pocket of her sweatshirt. "Not really. What's so great about getting a period?"

"It's not only about that. It's about—" What was it about, really? I stared down the street. "Not being left behind."

As soon as I said these words, my throat felt as if I'd swallowed something hard, like sea glass. That was it: I felt stranded. Like I was on a beach by myself, watching everybody swim away. Mom, Abi, Jules, Mak—

Marley frowned. "You think Abi and Jules and Mak are more mature than you? Just because they bleed once a month?"

"No," I admitted. "But it just feels like they're doing all this stuff, I don't know, *moving forward* without us. Doesn't it feel that way to you?"

"If it does, I don't care. Maybe I never wanted to be included with them in the first place."

I didn't know what to say to that. All this time I'd felt as if I were Marley's one true ally, the only one who was keeping her in the group, and she didn't even *want* to be included? "So can I ask you something? Why did you hang out with those guys if you hated it so much?"

"Because *you* were there, Lia. And we were friends."

"Were?"

She sighed. "Lia, I honestly don't know if I want to be

friends with you anymore. Not just because you lied so much. Because you do whatever Abi says."

Of everything she'd accused me of, this seemed the most unfair. "But that's not true! I challenge her all the time. I always stick up for you—"

"Yeah, thanks. I stick up for you too. And now we both don't have to anymore."

Some eighth-grade boys skateboarded past us. They looked like they were having good dumb fun, the way boys could.

Marley watched them, shielding her eyes from the sun. "I don't know, Lia—since the summer, it's like you've changed."

"Me? How can you say that, Marley? Except for you, I'm the only one of us who *hasn't* changed. That's *why* I lied!"

She shrugged. "Listen, I have a tutor coming, and my mom will kill me if I'm late, so . . ."

She reached into her jeans pocket. Then she held out a closed fist, as if she wanted me to guess what was in her hand.

"What is that?" I asked nervously.

"Just take them, okay?"

Her fist opened. But I didn't even have to look to know what they were.

The pieces of sea glass I'd given her at the end of the summer: green, ice blue, and white.

Apples and Oranges

ON TUESDAY MORNING MARLEY SPENT ALL OF homeroom sketching in her sketchbook. I didn't try to talk to her, because the truth was, I couldn't face her. She'd seen right through me all this time and she hadn't said a word about it—not to the other girls and not to me. Even though I didn't deserve it, I knew she'd been protecting me, or trying to. Until I guess she couldn't do it anymore, starting when Abi made her answer that dumb body-switching question.

But now I was worried about Marley. If she quit our

group, who were her friends? Where was she going to sit at lunch? Who would she hang out with after school and on weekends? Who would she send her turtle drawings to? She didn't have other friends in our grade, at least none I could name. It didn't seem fair that she should lose her whole social life over my stupid, selfish behavior. Even if she said she didn't want to be included, how could that possibly be true?

But that wasn't the only worry of the day. In PE I'd decided to change my clothes in front of my locker, because I knew if I hid in the bathroom again, Abi would drag me to her dermatologist after school. I slipped into my yoga pants, and just as I was changing into a dumb tee Aunt Shelby gave me (Honk if You're a Maine-iac), Abi came running over.

"Omigod," she said. "Jules had an accident!"

The word "accident" was not my favorite in the dictionary. My heart zoomed. "Should we call an ambulance?"

"No, no, not *that* kind of accident. A period accident." Abi's eyes were wide. "She wasn't expecting it today. And her pants are light blue."

"Oh."

"Yeah. She can't leave the bathroom like that, and she's too tiny to borrow Mak's gym pants or mine. So she needs yours, okay?"

"Sure. I'll keep on my yoga pants; she can have my jeans."

"And a pad?"

"What?"

"You know . . . a *pad*. Mak only has tampons for the pool, and Jules won't use them. You keep some extra pads in your locker, right?"

Um.

"Let me look," I said, rummaging through my messy locker. "Oh no. Sorry. I must have run out."

"Really? That's weird," Abi said.

What did she mean by that? Could she tell I was lying?

"Can't she borrow one of yours?" I asked, beginning to sweat.

"Nah, my period was last week; I didn't bring any new pads."

"Last week?"

"Huh?"

"Your period. I thought you said you got it over the weekend."

Abi's eyes flashed. "Are you serious, Lia? The weekend *is* last week; Monday is the start of the school week, right? And why are you arguing over something so ridiculous while Jules is in the bathroom freaking out?"

"Sorry," I said.

"Just give me the jeans, okay? I'll ask someone else."

"Try the gym office. Or the nurse," I suggested helpfully.

"Lia, I *know*," she growled.

By lunch, everything was back to normal. Except for the following:

1. Marley wasn't at our table. As far as I could tell, she wasn't even in the lunchroom.

2. Jules was wearing my jeans, which meant I was stuck in my sweaty yoga pants.

3. Abi *may* have figured out I'd been lying about my period.

4. Although she *may* have been lying about her own period. At least, that was a possibility, considering the way she'd lost track of the calendar.

5. She *may* have suspected that I suspected she was lying. And if she did, she was probably furious. Even *if* she'd been telling the truth.

Which explained the weird mood at the table as I sat down with my veggie pizza. Nobody was talking: Mak was reading her phone, Jules was nibbling chocolate chips off her cookie, and Abi was watching me with this twisted little smirk on her face.

Finally she said, "Hey, don't eat too much of that pizza, Lia. It has garlic."

"What's wrong with garlic?" I asked.

"Makes your breath stink. Then Graydon won't want to kiss you."

"Haha, really funny," I said. "And he definitely doesn't want to kiss me anyway."

"Sure he does," Mak said, suddenly looking up from her phone. "Come on, Lia. Everyone knows you guys have a giganto crush on each other."

"Excuse me, *what*?"

"It's not a secret, okay? He's always staring at you. And you're always turning all these crazy colors. Like right now."

There was no point denying the crazy-color part; I could tell my cheeks were blazing hot. And what was the point of denying the rest of it? I mean, if it was that obvious.

"Although, actually, I think he hates me," I said. "Or at the very least, he's been kind of avoiding me lately."

"Really? Why?" Jules asked sympathetically.

"I don't know. I tried to explain why Marley gave him that poem. It just came out wrong, I guess." I took another bite of pizza and thought about Marley, how much she'd put up with just to be my friend. "Can I ask you something, Abi? How come you dared Marley to give Graydon that poem? And then to kiss him?"

Abi laughed. "Because we knew she wouldn't."

"Why not?"

"Because *you* like him, doofus. But, of course, *you* wouldn't kiss him, either."

"Why wouldn't I?"

She rolled her eyes. "Oh, come on, Lia."

"Come on what?" I looked at Mak and Jules, but they were both watching Abi and me, like we were playing a ping-pong match. Her turn, my turn. "Come on *what*?" I repeated.

"Lia," Abi said. "You wouldn't kiss Graydon because you never kissed Tanner. You've never kissed *any* boy, right?"

"What? Where did you get that?"

"Oh, then you're saying it's true? You *did* kiss Tanner?"

"Abi, I told you—"

"Then prove it. Kiss Graydon."

"Are you joking? What does kissing Tanner have to do with—"

"Okay, fine, Lia. Then don't." Abi's voice was as sharp as a pair of scissors.

I was so mad I almost laughed.

And I knew I could get up from that table and storm off with my pizza. I didn't have to answer to Abi or take her obnoxious dare! Because that's what it was, a dare, even if we weren't playing the Truth or Dare game anymore.

But right away I thought this: If I stormed off the way

Marley had, I wouldn't be leaving all my friends behind—
it would be more like *they* were leaving *me*. And then I'd
be stranded on the beach without even Marley, just myself
and a bunch of reject sea glass.

Also, I couldn't help noticing how Jules and Mak were
eyeing me, like they were reading a book and wondering
what would happen next. Like I was probably just Poor
Nice Left-Behind Lia. But what if I wasn't? What if I could
surprise people—especially my friends? *What if everything about me was true?*

"All right," I said. "I'll do it."

Abi smiled in a way that made my insides twitch. "I
guess we'll have to see," she said.

The Kiss

THE QUESTION WAS WHERE TO DO THE KISS. IT had to be private enough for Graydon to feel as if his buddies wouldn't suddenly appear, but public enough for my friends to witness. I told myself that if I could just think of the perfect place at the perfect time, Graydon would probably let me kiss him. After all, he let me borrow his homework, and he'd asked me to dance that one time. He had to like me; if he didn't, he wouldn't have felt so bad about my role in the love poem prank.

As the afternoon passed, though, I was running out

of chances. I couldn't kiss him in math, because he sat at the Nerd Desk, in the front of the classroom. (I'd chosen a desk in the back, so I wouldn't be distracted too much by Mrs. Crawley's nose job.) In science he shared a lab station with Ben and Jake, and there was no way I'd do it in front of them. In English we had an in-class essay about *Roll of Thunder, Hear My Cry*, a book I liked, even though everyone else called it boring. And because I wanted to do a good job on the essay, I stayed in my seat an extra five minutes at the end of class, which meant I didn't see Graydon at his lockers at dismissal.

But I did catch up with him just before he got on the school bus.

"Graydon!" I called a few decibels too loudly.

He cringed. "Yeah?"

"Can I please talk to you? For a second?"

"Sure. What's up?"

This would have been the perfect opportunity to kiss him. Except none of my friends were there to witness it, so it wouldn't count.

"Graydon, I was wondering: Would you possibly like to go the diner? For a milk shake, maybe?"

"With you?" He squinted. Or maybe scowled.

I nodded.

"I dunno," he said. "I have a tutoring appointment."

"*You* get tutored?"

"No. I tutor Marley. In math. You didn't know?"

I shook my head.

"It isn't teaching her stuff; it's more like practicing. She's smart, but she needs to drill. And her mom pays ridiculously well."

I wondered if this was the "expensive tutor" Marley was always talking about.

"Anyway," I said. "We would be quick. So you can still be on time for your tutoring."

He blinked at me. "Well, I *am* kind of hungry," he admitted. "Sure, why not."

"I just need to do something first. Can you wait a sec?"

He unzipped his backpack and took out a book: *The Martian Chronicles.*

I ran inside the building. Abi, Mak, and Jules were still at their lockers.

"Okay," I said breathlessly. "Graydon and I are going to the diner. So can you meet us there? Well, not *meet* us; we'll need privacy. But I mean, can you guys go there? Now?"

Mak looked unsure. "I have to be back at the Y pool by three forty-five."

"It'll be fast," I promised.

Abi shrugged a yes. I didn't even wait for Jules's response; I knew that if Abi would do it, so would Jules.

I ran back outside to Graydon. It was a five-minute walk to the Maplebrook Diner, but Graydon was a surprisingly slow mover. I say "surprisingly" because everything about him was so quick and direct. Also, he didn't waste energy by talking. Mostly he listened while I described the plot of the HiberNation trilogy, which I'd just finished.

"And in the end Bree goes off on her own without an army?" he asked, just as we arrived at the diner. "That's slightly implausible, don't you think?"

"Not really. I thought the ending was cool."

"It may be *cool,* but it doesn't make any *sense.*"

Maggie the waitress walked over to us. "Same booth as usual?" she asked with a bored expression. I nodded. Although I immediately realized I'd made a mistake: Our regular booth was right by the door, so Graydon would be able to see my friends when they walked in. Also, when I kissed him, I didn't want the whole street to see.

"Can we please sit in the back instead?" I asked Maggie.

"I'm still your waitress wherever you park yourself, hon. Same order as usual? Chocolate shake?"

"Um, yes," I said as I slid into the seat facing the door. "Please."

"I'll have a chocolate chip hot fudge sundae with two squirts of whipped cream and *no* maraschino cherry," Graydon said.

Maggie rolled her eyes, like, *Great, another charming Maplebrook kid.*

"What's wrong with maraschino cherries?" I asked Graydon as soon as Maggie walked off.

"They're so uncherrylike," he answered. "They don't taste anything like real cherries—they just taste *red*-flavored. Just like 'grape flavor' tastes purple and 'blue raspberry' tastes blue. And of course there's no such thing as a 'blue raspberry,' anyway. . . ." He shook his head disgustedly.

"You should talk to Marley about fruit," I said. "She has this thing about raisins. All shriveled food, in fact."

"Shriveled food is *fine* with me. It's only *fake* food I object to."

I crossed my arms in front of my fake chest.

By now I'd run out of conversation. I kept glancing at the door, but my friends weren't walking in. If they didn't get here very soon, Graydon would leave for Marley's house. Finally Maggie showed up with our orders. She put Graydon's sundae in front of him. In front of me she put a cookie dough sundae with butterscotch syrup, whipped cream, and gummy bears.

Abi's usual, not mine. Maggie had gotten us mixed up.

"Wait," I protested. "I didn't order this."

"Yeah, I know, you're the chocolate shake," Maggie said. "Coming right up."

"But why did you bring me this?"

Maggie smirked. "It's a secret message from your secret admirer."

"What?"

"Look, that's what she told me to tell you, okay? You girls don't tip enough to make me deliver sundae-grams, or whatever that's supposed to be." Maggie walked off in a huff.

"You should read the napkin," Graydon said, swirling the hot fudge into his ice cream. "There appears to be writing."

I slipped the napkin out from under the parfait glass. Graydon was right. In letters smeary from the drips of butterscotch syrup and ice cream, there was a message, presumably for me: MEET IN BTHRM. NOW.

I crumpled the napkin. "Excuse me, Graydon. I have to go to the bathroom. I'll be right back," I mumbled.

"Take your time," he said, licking his spoon.

I speed-walked to the bathroom. Abi was waiting for me.

"You've been here the whole time?" I squeaked. "Where *are* you guys?"

"In the front. You walked right past us. So what's going on?"

"Now? I'm in the bathroom, talking to you."

"Haha." She checked out her sideways ponytail in the

mirror. "Well, hurry up! Mak has to leave."

"Abi, I can't just *attack* him. I haven't even gotten my milk shake yet!"

Abi raised an eyebrow. "You need a milk shake before you kiss a boy? Is that how it went with Tanner?"

"What? No. There were no milk shakes; we were on a beach, remember? And truthfully, Abi, I don't appreciate being pressured."

"No one is *pressuring* you, Lia. If you don't want to kiss Graydon—"

A stall opened. Out came Ruby Lewis. "Hey, guys," she said.

Oh, perfect. She'd heard the whole thing!

"*Hi.*" Abi greeted her with a weird sort of cheeriness. "Don't you love these mirrors? You can really get a sense of *how you look* in them."

"Yeah, that's usually how it goes with mirrors," I muttered. "We should leave, Abi."

"Wait a sec. I want to see how I look *from different angles.*" Abi turned to the left and pretended to inspect her profile. Then she turned to the right. "Oh good, I'm *all tucked in.*"

Ruby soaped her hands in the sink. "Yeah, don't worry. You look fine. Bye, Abi."

"See you," Abi said.

"That was subtle," I murmured as we left the bathroom.

"You think?" Abi asked, laughing. "Maybe I should go back in there and do jumping jacks or something. Joking," she added, when she saw my horrified expression.

I let Abi return to her table first, then I slid back into my seat. While I'd been in the bathroom, Maggie had taken away the sundae and delivered my chocolate shake instead.

I took an extra-long sip of it. The sweet coldness numbed my brain, and I felt grateful.

"Everything okay?" Graydon asked. By then his sundae was just a small puddle in the bottom of his bowl.

"Yep," I answered.

"You got everything straightened out? Synchronized your watches?"

"Excuse me?"

"With your friends, I mean."

I looked up at him.

"Your *friends* are here," he said, as if I'd been in a coma. "In the diner."

"They are? Huh." I sipped more milk shake. "Well, everybody's here today. There's Ruby. Oh, hi, Ruby!"

I waved to Ruby as she exited the bathroom. She gave me a look, like, *Lia, did you forget you saw me thirty seconds ago?*

"I meant your other friends," Graydon said. "Abigail,

Julianna, and Makayla. It's so funny that they just happen to be here right now."

"I know, right? What a coincidence." My heart was banging. *Kiss him already. Go.* "So, Graydon. There was something I wanted to ask you."

"Yeah? Shoot."

I took one more huge sip of milk shake. I wiped my mouth with a napkin—but not completely, so my lips would taste chocolaty. "I was wondering—would it be okay if I please kissed you?"

He pushed away his empty sundae glass. "No, actually."

NO? HE SAID NO?

OMIGOD, HE SAID NO.

FLOOR, JUST SWALLOW ME WHOLE.

"Nothing personal," he explained. "I'm just not kissing you in front of your friends."

"But—"

"I'm not stupid, Lia. This is obviously a part of that game you're playing, and I refuse to let you all make fun of me. Again."

I was probably dripping quarts of sweat into my milk shake, but I didn't care. "Oh, but we're not playing that game anymore!"

"Right."

"No, I swear!"

"Really? Then why the sudden invitation? And why did your friends just happen to be here? And why did I see Abi coming out of the bathroom just before you?"

"Graydon, really, I really do like you. I promise. They couldn't make me kiss you if I didn't!"

"Too bad for you, then." He reached into his wallet for a five-dollar bill and tossed it onto the table. "I don't get why you hang out with those girls, anyway."

"They're my friends," I said weakly.

"Yeah, you think so, Lia? Anyhow, thanks for telling me about that book. I might read it, even with the dumb ending."

As soon as Graydon was out the door, Abi, Jules, and Mak came running over.

"What happened?" Jules asked. Her eyes were popping.

I winced. "Nothing. Didn't you see?"

"We sure did," Abi said cheerfully. "You never kissed."

"But it's totally unfair!" I shouted it so loudly an old lady at the next booth frowned at me. So I lowered my voice. "The only reason we didn't was because Abi sent over that stupid sundae. It made him suspicious!"

"Well, what were we supposed to do?" Abi argued. "We can't text you if you don't have a phone!"

"Why did you need to text me, anyway?"

"Because Mak has to leave for swim practice now,"

Jules said. "And we all wanted to see." She put her hand on my shoulder as if she were consoling me. "You'll do it some other time, Lia, okay?"

The three of them left while I pretended to finish my shake. Things were just getting worse and worse. Marley had stopped being my friend. Graydon pretty much hated me now; at the absolute least, he didn't trust me. Abi was on the warpath, and Mak and Jules were just going along with whatever she did. I was hanging on to my group of friends by a thread—and the truth was, I didn't even know why I wanted to be friends with them anymore.

Honey

WHEN I GOT HOME ABOUT AN HOUR LATER, VAL'S car was in my driveway. As soon as she saw me, she got out of her car with three full shopping bags. *Oh, right. Today is Tuesday.*

"There you are," she said brightly. "I was starting to worry. And I would have called you, but—"

I threw away my phone. "Sorry," I said. "I should have told you I wouldn't be coming straight home."

"No problem. I have a PTA meeting later, so I

thought I'd bring your meal a bit earlier than usual. Can I come in?"

Dang. I'd hoped she'd just give me the shopping bags and drive off. Then I immediately scolded myself for being so ungrateful. "Oh, of course."

She followed me into the kitchen, explaining all the food she'd brought: the chicken stew that needed reheating, the small rolls that needed defrosting, the salad that needed tossing, the lemon cake that needed refrigerating. We emptied two of the bags.

That left a third bag.

"May I sit a moment?" she asked, taking the third bag with her.

I sat; she sat.

"This other bag is for you, honey." She pushed the bag over to my feet.

Inside were six packages of size regular no-wings maxi pads.

"Val," I said, swallowing, "thank you. But you really didn't have to—"

"No, no, it's completely my pleasure."

I stared at the pads. Abi must have told her I didn't have any pads left in my PE locker—that was the only explanation. But if she had told Val, that had to mean she *didn't* think I was lying, right? She had to believe I'd run out of pads because I *used* them. So maybe she didn't believe I'd kissed Tanner, but how much of the My First Period story *did* she believe? It was hard to keep track of all the details.

"Lia, are you okay?" Val asked.

"Yes, fine. I was just thinking."

"About what? You can tell me, honey."

I blinked at her. Mom used to call me "honey." Dad was "baby" and Nate was "sweetie," but I was always "honey."

Suddenly all I wanted was for Val to stay in that chair calling me "honey."

"Marley's not our friend anymore," I blurted. *Oh great, why did I tell her* that?

Val's forehead puckered. "Really? Did you girls have a fight?"

The way she said this, I could tell that she was hearing about it for the first time.

"Not exactly," I said. "It's a little complicated."

"Well." Val sighed. "I'm sorry to hear that. Marley is a very sweet girl."

"Oh, she's better than 'a sweet girl.' She's the coolest one of us all, and I think we were horrible to her."

"You girls couldn't possibly be horrible," Val argued.

Was she serious? I almost laughed. "Oh, we could, believe me."

"But what caused it? Did something happen?"

"Nothing specific. Sometimes people bully for no reason."

I knew I should've just stopped right there—but it was like I was a toddler in a stroller and Mom—or was it Aunt Shelby?—was pushing me from behind. I had no control; I couldn't steer. I was just going forward.

"Like when you bullied my aunt," I said. "I mean, was that really for a reason?"

Val's eyes widened in shock. "Excuse me?"

"Aunt Shelby said you bullied her in middle school."

Val's face had turned white. "Shelby said that?"

"Yes. She said you put stuff in her gym locker."

"Stuff?"

"Baby stuff, like undershirts. Because she was flat. And you called her names."

Val shook her mom-ponytail. Her mouth was tight. "Well, I'm sorry she remembers it that way. If it happened, and I'm not saying it did, I honestly have no memory of it. It was a very long time ago, Lia."

She stood up to leave.

"Thanks for the food," I said quickly. "And for everything. Maybe you should keep some pads for Abi?"

"Abi doesn't need any yet. Have a good night, Lia." She turned and let herself out.

Whoa. So I *was* right about Abi, after all. Half of me wanted to do a victory dance or something, because I'd figured out Abi's secret on my own.

But the other half of me—the other two-thirds, really— just felt quaky about what I'd said to Val.

What was wrong with me? What had I just done?

The Extra Pillow

ABI WAS WAITING FOR ME OUTSIDE HOMEROOM the next morning. The fact that she was on her own, not with Jules and Mak for once, made my heart thud.

"Lia, we need to talk," she said quietly. "Did you say anything to my mom yesterday?"

"About what?"

"About *anything*. Take a guess."

"You mean about being mean to Marley? I told her it was *all* of us."

"Yeah? Then why did she blame *me*?"

"I don't know, Abi. I swear."

"You're such a liar, aren't you? Lia the Liar." She narrowed her eyes. "Mom *also* said you were rude to her."

"I'm sorry. I didn't mean to be." I could tell how lame that sounded, so I added, "It was just something to do with my aunt."

"What I don't understand," Abi said, her voice getting dangerously loud, "is how you could treat my mom *rudely* when she cooked for your family *every week for the past two years*. There were times I was even a bit jealous about it, to be honest, because she was so busy shopping and cooking for *you,* she couldn't do things with *me*."

"I'm sorry, Abi. We're all so grateful. We kept telling her she didn't need to, but she—"

"She felt *bad* for you, Lia!" Abi's mouth hung open. "Everybody did. Can't you understand that?"

My throat burned. "I really don't want you guys feeling bad for me."

"Well, too bad, because everybody does! But that doesn't give you the right to go around stealing other people's moms. And then being *rude* about it."

Now my eyes were stinging. "Abi, I'd never steal your mom from you; that's impossible. I'm really, really sorry if you feel—"

"And saying Mom should take care of Ruby too, like

she has nothing else to do! You know what? I don't know what else to say to you, Lia. I'm sick of listening to all your lies. Don't bother sitting with us at lunch, all right?"

Somehow I made it to the nurse's office. As soon as I walked in the door, Mrs. Garcia got off her phone. "You okay, Lia?"

I shook my head. I couldn't talk without crying.

She led me to a cot behind a blue curtain. At the beginning of fifth grade, which was just a few months after the Accident, Mrs. Garcia told me I could come there whenever I wanted. She said I didn't need to feel sick; sometimes kids who'd "been through something" needed a quiet place during the day, she told me. If I wanted to talk to her, or to the school psychologist, I could; but if I just wanted to hang out with her for a bit, that was okay too.

So I came there a lot in fifth grade. By sixth grade, I came maybe three or four times the entire year.

This was the first time I'd come in seventh grade. Nothing had changed. The same posters on the walls (EAT A RAINBOW OF FOODS; HANDWASHING IS THE BEST DEFENSE), the same antiseptic-spray smell, the same thin mattresses on the metal cots.

"Would you like an extra pillow?" Mrs. Garcia asked.

She remembered I'd always asked for one; for a second she reminded me of Maggie at the diner ("The usual?"). I nodded. Mrs. Garcia brought me the pillow. Then she pulled up a chair to the cot.

"What is it, dear? You look pale. Anything hurt?"

I put my hand on my stomach.

"Okay. Mind if I take your temp?" She didn't wait for my answer. "Ninety-eight point eight. Can you tell me what the pain feels like?"

"Cramps." It seemed like the safest choice.

She nodded understandingly. "Ah. Have you started menstruating yet?"

I shook my head.

"Your body may be getting ready, then. Would you like a Tylenol?"

"No thanks. Can I ask you something?"

"Of course."

"Why does it have to hurt?"

Mrs. Garcia smiled kindly. "Well, you remember from health class, Lia: a girl gets her period when her ovaries—"

"That's not really what I meant," I interrupted.

"Ah." She thought a minute. "I guess it has to hurt so you pay attention. If it didn't hurt, you might not notice when things were happening."

"What's so great about noticing? I think I'd rather *not*

notice. Maybe I could just hibernate or something."

She smiled. "Oh, I doubt that. You don't want to sleep through your life, do you?"

"No," I admitted. "I guess not." The bell rang for first period. I could hear doors opening, kids spilling into the halls, calling to one another, laughing. "Mrs. Garcia?"

"Yes, dear?"

"Can I please just stay here a little while? For my cramps."

"Of course. As long as you need."

"Thank you." Suddenly something occurred to me. "Can I ask you a favor?"

"Always, Lia."

"Would you please talk to Ruby Lewis? She needs to wear a bra, or people will keep making fun of her."

Mrs. Garcia tried to be cool about it, but I could tell her ears were perking up. "Oh, really? Anyone in particular?"

"No! Just basically everyone."

"All right, will do."

"Thanks. And please don't tell her I told you. It'll just embarrass her."

"Not how I roll," she said, winking.

Amethysts

THAT EVENING DINNER WAS *LEFTOVERS: THE Return of Val's Chicken Stew.* But I was sure it was actually *Food From Val: The Final Installment.* Because after the way I'd accused Val yesterday and the way Abi reacted at school today, I was positive we wouldn't be getting any more meal deliveries on Tuesdays.

So I felt guilty. Dad and Nate were obviously enjoying every bite, and because I'd opened my big mouth, I'd be depriving them of the highlight of the food week.

"You okay, Lee-lee?" Dad asked as he mopped up some chicken stew gravy with a roll.

"Why are you asking?" I said.

"Because you've barely touched your food. And you didn't eat last night, either."

Nate looked up. "You'd better not be dieting, Fungus Face."

"I told you I wasn't, Fungus Breath!" I snapped.

"*Okay*," Dad said. "So what's up? I had a call from Mrs. Garcia. She said you weren't feeling well at school."

"I'd rather not talk about it."

"All right."

Dad kept eating. Was that it, then? *I'd rather not talk about it. All right.* That's all it took? With Mom I'd never get off as easily, that was for sure.

But it didn't work with Dad, either. He just waited for Nate to finish eating and excuse himself to do homework.

Then he said, "Oh, by the way, Lia. Something came for you in today's mail." Dad handed me a small box addressed to AMALIA JESSICA ROLLINS. It had a return address of SHELBY HEYWOOD, BENCHLEY, MAINE. Not even a street.

"I'll open it later," I muttered. Knowing my aunt, it was probably some humiliating undergarment.

Dad pushed away his plate. "So I've been thinking,

Lee-lee. You're at an age when it's really hard not to have your mom around. You probably have lots of stuff going on that you feel you can't share with me."

Uh-oh. We were going to talk about *those* things.

"Is that right?" he asked gently.

"Maybe. Yeah." I bit my pointer nail.

"I want you to know that I'm always here for you. But in case you'd rather talk to a female adult—"

Blerg. "Female adult." As opposed to "woman."

"—I hope you'll talk to that nice nurse at school. Or to Val. Or your aunt."

Aunt Shelby only won the bronze, I noticed. "Not Val, okay?"

"No? How come?"

"Because Abi hates me."

"Why do you say that?"

"Because she thinks I'm ungrateful. Also a liar."

"You?"

"Yeah. Because I am."

"Lia." Dad reached across the table to squeeze my arm. "I don't know what this is about, but whatever happened between you girls, you're not a liar. You're the most honest person I know. And your aunt agrees."

"Aunt Shelby?"

He nodded. "She didn't go into details about this summer, but she did mention that you have a highly developed set of ethics."

Blerg. "Developed."

And I couldn't imagine my aunt using the expression "set of ethics." Probably she was referring to my horror at her fake unicorn root. Or about being spied on by Agent Yazmin. Or about the padding, which was now pretending to be my chest.

Dad was searching my face. "So if it's something you ever want to talk to me about, I'd love to listen. Even if it's a woman thing or a body thing—"

I kissed his cheek before he could finish. "Thanks, Dad," I said. "I love you."

His face relaxed. "Love you too, Lee-lee."

Upstairs in my bedroom, with my door closed, I opened the package from Aunt Shelby. Inside was a plastic bag containing three purple crystals and a typed note on a strip of paper: *Amethysts are master healing crystals that provide protection during periods of transition. They support those who may be experiencing loss. They boost production of hormones and relieve stress. They can stimulate insight and help with decision-making and motivation.*

Also there was a note from Aunt Shelby:

Dear Lia,

I hope you like these amethysts—I picked them out with YOU in mind. They're most powerful if you keep them next to your heart. (Do you have a locket? Or maybe a shirt with a chest pocket?) If you have trouble sleeping, put them under your pillow.

Hope to see you again very soon!

Love,

Aunt S

PS. All cats say: HELLO, but a special MEOW from Escobar and Doomhammer. And a purr from Stinkbug, who is sitting on my head.

I reread the note about amethysts, wondering if my aunt actually believed in all that magic crystal stuff. Maybe she thought if I slipped one of these purple crystals into the padding of my bra, or turned it into a decoration between the cups, like the rhinestone, I'd feel better about losing Mom, not to mention all my friends. And maybe she thought my hormones would be motivated to start women-struating. Or something.

Because, as we all agreed, she was crazy.

The amethysts were pretty, though. I loved how rough they were, like purple icebergs, and how they changed when you held them to the light. All my best collections were like that—always there, always the same, but different every time you looked at them.

Well, I told myself, if Aunt Shelby ever did open that Herb 'n' Legend store, I might start a stone-and-crystal collection. Agates and jaspers and quartzes, maybe others. That would definitely be a cool collection, even if they didn't have magical powers.

Despite the fact that I wasn't sleepy, I crawled into bed. I pulled out some bins from underneath the mattress—the sea glass, the shells, and the marbles. And instead of doing homework, or reading, or calling my ex-friends, or calling Val, or calling my aunt, or figuring out how I was going to survive all the hundreds of days left of school and all the millions of days left without a mom or any friends, I organized my collections until I fell asleep.

Girl Protectors

WELL, AT LEAST I DON'T HAVE TO WEAR PADDED bras anymore.

That was my first thought when I woke up the next morning, still dressed in my clothes from Wednesday. Now that I was officially friendless, I didn't need to fool anyone anymore. Even the boy I liked hated me, so who would peek at my nonexistent chest? Nobody. Woo-hoo, right?

I pulled off yesterday's bra, tossed it into my closet, and put on Nate's baggy old Maplebrook High School tee, with nothing underneath. Everything would be so much simpler now, I told myself. All I needed to do was get through school with no drama. Just keep my head down and take notes. And when it was three o'clock, run.

That was my plan. And it worked great too—through homeroom, art, and French. But then PE happened, and everything fell apart.

For starters, I got to the locker room a minute late, because Mademoiselle Schecter, the French teacher, wanted to chat with me about the fact that I hadn't turned in Thursday's homework. She was so sweet about it, looking into my eyes with so much understanding and concern that I almost burst into tears. I didn't, but by the time I got to the gym locker room, I was still a little shaky.

And when I got to my locker, I saw that someone had taped a sign to the door:

LIAR.

Right away I recognized Abi's handwriting. I ripped it down without saying a word, changed into my yoga pants, crumpled the note into my pants pocket, and took my place on the gym floor for attendance.

We were still on the volleyball unit. The second I lined up for Team A, Abi, Mak, and Jules walked across the net to join Team B.

Who cares? Who cares? I chanted in my head. We played for about five minutes. The score was tied 1–1. When it was my turn to serve, I didn't score a point, but I hit the ball okay. In fact, well enough for Ruby to high-five me, despite the invisible sign I wore around my neck: NO ATTENTION, PLEASE—THE MANAGEMENT.

"Nice serve, Lia," Ruby said.

"Thanks," I said, looking at her from the neck upward.

Then it was Mak's turn to serve. When she bounced the ball a few times, she looked dangerous, as if she had a strategy. Maybe she did, I thought, because suddenly she hit it—*thwunk!*—straight at my chest.

I screamed.

Abi laughed.

The pain was sharp—hot and tingling, not like anything I'd ever felt before. But even as I felt it, even as it took my breath away, I thought: *That laugh belonged to Abi.* No one else had a laugh like punctuation. Like a combination question mark and exclamation point: *Omigod, did you see THAT?!*

"Sorry," Mak called out. I ignored her, yelling at myself not to cry in front of my ex-friends, whatever it took.

Ms. Bivens, the gym teacher, came running over. "Lia, are you okay?"

"Fine," I muttered.

She put her hands on my shoulders. "Never say you're fine when you're not. Come with me."

She led me to the sideline. "Well? What happened?"

I could have said something like, *Oh, I just screamed in agony because our team messed up, and you know how intense I get about volleyball, Ms. Bivens*. But I couldn't lie. When the volleyball hit my chest, it knocked the invisible sign from my neck. And even if it hadn't, Abi's laugh had made me furious. I refused to pretend I hadn't heard it. So I told Ms. Bivens what happened.

She frowned. "Does your chest still hurt?"

I shook my head.

"But your feelings?"

I shrugged.

"Abi and Mak, could you please step over here for a moment?" she called loudly.

"Ms. Bivens," I begged, "please don't—"

She blew her whistle. "Let's go, girls. *Now*."

"But I'm about to serve," Abi protested.

"It can wait."

Abi and Mak exchanged glances. I thought I saw Mak mumble something and Abi shrug in response as they walked over.

"Ms. Bivens, it was an accident," Mak said immediately. "I'd never hit anyone on purpose. And if my serve hurt you, Lia, I'm really sorry." Her face looked pinched in a way I could tell meant she wasn't lying.

I nodded. "Okay."

Ms. Bivens seemed satisfied. "All right, Makayla, you can get back on the court now. Abi, why did you laugh?"

Abi blinked. "I don't know. When Lia screamed, it just surprised me, I guess."

"That's not true," I snapped. "You laughed because you thought it was funny."

Her eyes widened. "I did not."

"You also put this on my locker, didn't you?" I yanked the crumpled paper from my pants pocket. "A sign that says 'Liar'?"

"It doesn't say 'Liar.' It just says your name. 'Lia R.'"

"Oh, come on," I said scornfully. "Why would you put my name on my locker? Just to be *nice*?"

"Someone wanted to give you a note, and they asked which was your locker. I can't help it if your name is Lia R."

"Abi, that is such a bunch of—"

"It was Graydon." She smirked. "It was a love poem."

"It was not! Don't lie!"

"Hold it right there, girls," Ms. Bivens ordered. If she could have blown her whistle at us, she would have. "This is sounding like a personal conflict, not a gym issue. If you can't resolve it yourselves, I suggest you take it to a guidance counselor. All I want to say here is that in *my* gym, we don't laugh at a classmate's injury. Understood, Abi?"

Abi nodded, but her lips were tight.

"All right, then. Return to the game."

As Abi jogged off, Ms. Bivens turned to me. "Simple suggestion for you: sports bra. To protect your girls." She gestured at my chest.

"Oh, but I don't have—I mean, I don't need a bra."

"Don't be too sure, Lia. I know that scream when I hear it."

At home that afternoon, I locked myself in the upstairs bathroom. I pulled off all my clothes and took inventory.

No visible hair anywhere. No waist or hips.

But were breasts finally happening? I wasn't sure; it's not like I'd suddenly come down with a bad case of cleavage. But if I stood sideways and held my breath, I thought I *might* be seeing some faint puffiness. Maybe. Possibly. And if I were, it would explain why the volleyball pain had been so . . . painful.

Did I actually need some girl protectors, after all?

Huh, I thought.

Maybe I did.

Dark Cloud

DINNER THAT NIGHT WAS SPAGHETTI AND SALAD, which Nate and I made together while Dad grated some parmesan cheese and set the table. The three of us had just sat down to start eating when the kitchen phone rang.

We looked at each other. When Mom was here, she refused to let us answer the phone at dinnertime. *It's probably just a telemarketer,* she would say. *If it was a real person, then he or she should learn to respect our dinner hour!*

Did we really spend an entire hour eating dinner with

her every night? I couldn't remember. We always did start the meal at the same time, though—six thirty. These days we ate when Dad got home, sometimes at six, sometimes as late as seven forty-five. Dad said that since we were so unpredictable with our meal schedule, it didn't seem fair to punish people who wanted to talk to us, so he always answered the phone.

While Dad spoke quietly to the caller, Nate and I ate our spaghetti, not talking so we could eavesdrop. Finally Dad said, "I'll put her on." Then he handed me the phone.

My heart bounced. Who could possibly be calling *me*? "Hello?" I asked.

"Niecelet!" Aunt Shelby shouted. "Bad me for ruining your dinner! How *are* you?"

I told her it was fine; I was fine; everyone in the family was fine. By the time she'd told me about the cats (all were great, except Stinkbug, who had a nail infection, which she was treating with a special cat-foot herb she'd read about online), I was upstairs in my bedroom with the door shut.

"So listen to *this*," Aunt Shelby said breathlessly. "Guess who called me today!"

I told her I couldn't guess, so she might as well just tell me.

"Vaaaaal," she said, as if the name had three syllables.

"*What?*"

"Yep. She said you'd accused her of torturing me in middle school?"

"Omigod. I never said torture, I swear!"

My aunt laughed. "Relax, buttercup. She actually called me to *apologize*. She said she didn't remember the locker room business when you first mentioned it, but the more she thought about it, the more it came back to her and the more she realized how hurtful she'd been back then. Can you believe it?"

"No," I answered truthfully. Then I added, "Although Val can be really nice sometimes."

"Well, she couldn't have been nicer on the phone today! So apparently it *is* possible to outgrow the Mean Girl routine!" Aunt Shelby laughed again. "And afterward we had a wonderful conversation. Did you know she's into crystals?"

"No, I didn't."

"I even told her about my stores. She seemed really interested. I'm thinking of asking her to invest in Herb 'n' Legend, because I'm pretty sure your dad's not gonna."

"Awesome."

Aunt Shelby paused. "Okay, buttercup, what's wrong?"

"Nothing."

"Don't lie to your aunt. Something's up; I can hear it in your voice."

I chewed the inside of my cheek. "It's no big deal. I've just lost every single one of my friends. Including Abi."

"You did? When? What happened?"

I suddenly realized how exhausted I was. Not talking, keeping your head down, took effort. Almost as much effort as telling lies and keeping your stories straight.

So I told her everything: about the Truth or Dare game, and Abi constantly fighting with Mak, and Marley quitting the game and also our group. About the fake My First Period story. About the LIA R sign and how Abi laughed when the volleyball hit my girls. Even the part about fake-kissing Tanner. Even the part about not kissing Graydon.

Aunt Shelby listened without interrupting. When I finished, she said, "All right, Lia. Here's what you're going to do. Invite your friends—just those four girls—to your house on Saturday. Say it's your birthday party."

"But that's ridiculous. My birthday isn't until April, and they all know it!"

"Say it's an early birthday. Or a half birthday. Or an anti-birthday. I'll bake a cake. What kind would they like?"

"Chocolate," I said immediately. "Like the kind Val made us as cupcakes. But what's the point of inviting them to *anything*? I told you they *hate* me. They won't come!"

"Oh, yes, they will. I'll talk to Val, my new best friend."

That was too warped for my brain to process. "Okay, but even if they *do* come, the thing is, I'm not sure I *want* to be friends with them after all the stuff that's happened."

"Buttercup, let me share a little wisdom. In life, it's so important to get things out in the bright sunshine, share your feelings, come to a mutual understanding, and then move on. Otherwise all that negative energy just sits like a dark cloud over your universe. Look at Val and me."

Was she joking? "Aunt Shelby, you *didn't* share your feelings with Val! For *twenty-five years*! I shared them *for* you!"

"And I'm deeply grateful, Lia. I feel like you made the sun come out for us. But now it's my turn to be there for *you*."

I bit a hangnail on my pinkie. "What will you do?"

"Don't worry. I have an idea."

"Okay, but what is it?"

"It's a whole creative process. I'm still feeling it out."

"Aunt Shelby—"

"You just leave it to me, niecelet. I'll see you tomorrow night!"

I guessed that Dad thought I was talking to my aunt about bras or bobby pins or something equally girly, because he let me stay on the phone for more than an hour. When I hung up he didn't ask me what we discussed; he nuked my spaghetti in the microwave and even let me take it up to my room.

But I couldn't eat.

The relief I'd felt evaporated almost immediately. What exactly would my crazy aunt do? How exactly would she solve all my problems? Even *she* admitted she always "messed up" when it came to "daughter stuff," so it was hard for me to trust her, especially with a situation this hopeless. And the party idea made zero sense. I couldn't imagine even sitting in same living room as my ex-friends—any of them, including Marley.

And speaking of Marley: If Aunt Shelby asked her new BFF, Val the Former Bully, to force Abi, Jules, and Mak to show up, that wouldn't mean a thing to Marley. If this party was seriously going to happen, I'd need to invite Marley on my own.

But first I'd need to think of a reason for her to accept.

Seashells

HOW DO YOU INVITE FRIENDS WHO AREN'T YOUR friends to a party that isn't a party? That you don't know anything about? That you're not even sure *you* want to go to?

I sat at my desk for almost an hour, puzzling it out. I couldn't just text everyone since I didn't have a phone, and even if I borrowed Nate's, texting seemed kind of weird if we weren't talking. Plus, texts were easy to ignore, and I probably should know who (if anyone) was coming.

It occurred to me that I could make a big-deal invitation if I used a few of my five hundred name labels:

Amalia Jessica Rollins requests the honor of your presence—

But that sounded too wedding-y. And too dress-uppy. Better to make it sound ultracasual:

> Please come to a thing
> Where: Here
> When: Sat @ 6 p.m.
> Why: Not sure. Something about dark
> clouds in the universe?

Finally I gave up trying to do invitations. I just wrote *Lia's, Sat @ 6 p.m.* on four small strips of paper, each about the size of a cookie fortune, and stuffed the strips into seashells from my collection. I had no choice but to give these out tomorrow, because tomorrow was Friday, and this party-ish event was happening Saturday.

The next morning outside homeroom, I gave Mak a seashell.

"There's something inside," I told her.

She looked grossed out.

"Don't worry; it's not alive," I explained.

I watched her pull out the fortune-cookie strip.

She read it, frowned, then looked up at me. "You know, Lia, I really didn't mean to hit you with that ball."

"I know."

"And I'm still so mad at Abi for laughing."

"Me too." Then I stopped myself. For all I knew, Mak and Abi could be having one of their five-minute feuds; it would be pointless to get in the middle of it. "So you'll come?"

"Yeah, why not." She didn't say anything else, or ask any questions about my mystery gathering, which was kind of funny; I mean, I could have been inviting her over to floss teeth. On the other hand, "yeah, why not" counted as a yes, which was the main thing.

I decided to invite Jules and Abi together. Jules would follow Abi's lead in any direction; if Abi was coming (because Val forced her), so would Jules. If Abi refused to come (because she hated me for all eternity), neither would Jules—although she'd probably act all sweet and sorry.

After French, I hurried to PE. I stood in front of Jules's gym locker with the seashells poking out of the pocket of my yoga pants. Finally they both showed up in matching sideways ponytails.

"Can I give you guys something?" I asked. Not waiting

for an answer, I handed them seashells. I'd been wondering if Mak had texted them during the morning, or met them for a secret rendezvous to warn them I was distributing shells—but by the startled looks on their faces, I could tell she hadn't. "There's a note inside," I explained.

Jules dug it out with her fingernail. "What is this, like, a party?"

"Exactly—it's *like* a party," I answered. "Can you come?"

She glanced at Abi, who shrugged sullenly.

"Will there be chocolate?" Jules asked.

"Ridiculous amounts."

Jules smiled. "Sure, we'll come. Thanks, Lia."

Abi glared at me, but she didn't contradict Jules. Obviously, Aunt Shelby had spoken to Val, and Val had scolded Abi, although who knew about what.

So that meant three ex-friends were coming. Woo-hoo. Marley was going to be the hardest to invite. For one thing, I didn't know her schedule—she was in my homeroom but not in any of my classes, and sometimes she worked in the Resource Room with an aide or a special ed teacher.

Plus, she hadn't spoken to me since the day of Abi's "fun" body-switching question. I knew it was stupid, but I'd kind of thought she'd slip me a drawing—maybe that fantasy tree I'd admired in her sketchpad—as a way of making up after all the upsetting stuff she'd said. But she hadn't. She didn't make eye contact with me in homeroom or in the hallway. Once I saw her after school walking in the direction of the diner, so I waved—but I couldn't tell if she waved back, or was just pushing her bangs out of her eyes.

Still, I told myself, Marley had only said she "didn't know" if she wanted to be friends—which meant that *possibly* there was a *slight* chance she'd show up at my sort-of-party. Anyway, if we weren't friends, we couldn't be non-friends even worse than now—so there was nothing to lose by handing her a seashell, right?

Since Graydon tutored Marley, I thought he might know where to find her. He and his friends played their card game in the computer lab during lunch sometimes, so I went there as soon as I'd grabbed a yogurt from the cafeteria. And to my shock, there was Marley—in the computer lab—playing the Phantom game with Graydon, Ben, and Jake.

"I AM INVINCIBLE," she shouted, slamming a card on the table.

"Yeah, yeah," Ben said impatiently. "Your turn, Gray."

Graydon looked up. "Hey," he said, seeing me standing by the door. "You wanna play, Lia?"

"No. I mean no, thanks," I said hurriedly. "Marley, can I talk to you a second?"

"Now?" She frowned.

"When you're finished?"

"Sure. First I have to annihilate these miserable wretches with my cunning gamesmanship."

"Shut up and play," Graydon muttered.

I sat there, eating my yogurt and watching the game. As far as I could tell, Marley was dominating.

Finally she shouted, "VICTORY!", stood, and did a sort of spazzy touchdown dance that was mainly just flapping her elbows and twirling in a circle. My first reaction was, *Good thing Abi isn't here to see this.* My second was, *So what if she were?*

When Marley finished, she came over to me with a grin so wide I could see her green and orange rubber bands.

"You really rock at that game," I said.

"Yeah, I do," she stated, as if it were just a fact. "So what did you want to talk to me about?"

I handed her a seashell. "Can you come?"

She ran her fingers through her messy bangs.

"I really hope you can," I added.

"I dunno, Lia. Who else is coming?"

"Well, our other ex-friends."

"Our?"

"Yeah, I'm not friends with them either now."

"Huh." She nodded thoughtfully. "Why are you inviting them, then?"

"It's more like my aunt is."

"Your *aunt*?"

"Yeah, I don't get it either. She refuses to tell me what she's planning. It'll be something weird, though."

"Weird how?"

I rolled my eyes. "She's into botanicals and soup and crystals, so it could be anything. And she has these theories about clouds and, I don't know, negative energy in the universe."

"I'm sorry, what?"

"Yeah, I know. I don't get it either."

"Well, it doesn't sound like another boring pizza-and-bowling party. But . . ." She shrugged.

"Marley, *please* come. I'm begging you. I need you there for sanity."

"That's a nice compliment," she said quietly. "Thank you."

"Plus, there'll be chocolate," I added.

She sighed. "All right. I'll come. But I have to warn you, Lia: If anyone picks on me, I'm fighting back."

"Good. Me too."

Marley returned to her game. I could have gone to the cafeteria then, but I stayed in the computer lab, watching them play.

One Big Circle

WHEN AUNT SHELBY DROVE UP THAT EVENING in her rusty old pickup, all she'd tell me was that she had "stuff planned" and tomorrow was "going to be awesome," and I should "just try to relax." But relaxing was out of the question. Ever since the Accident, I hadn't been a huge fan of surprises. For me to relax, I needed to know details. And the more Aunt Shelby refused to answer my questions, the more unrelaxed I felt.

At breakfast early Saturday morning, she suggested a distraction: bra shopping. At first I thought she was joking.

"You mean you really want some *blueberry pancakes*, right?" I said.

"Okay, I deserved that," Aunt Shelby admitted, smiling. "But this time, Lia, no fibbing. I promise."

I thought about it. "I don't know. Last time you forced me to get what *you* wanted."

She clasped her hands on her chest. "I won't even come inside the store. You can get whatever you want. Within my budget, of course."

I almost said no. But then I remembered about the volleyball incident and Ms. Bivens recommending a sports bra for my "girls." I also considered my maybe-possible boob sighting in the bathroom mirror. Plus, I could see that my aunt was trying to make up for stuff. And if I could shop at Shy Violet's without her interference . . . I said yes.

By ten o'clock we were at the mall. Aunt Shelby had brought along her laptop so she'd have something to do while I was inside the store. I watched her sit herself on a bench, open her computer, and then just space out looking at three teen girls who were debating Starbucks versus Dunkin' Donuts.

Something weird must have happened to my brain, because I decided to ask her to help me shop.

"Niecelet, I think I'm going to cry," she said. I could see she meant it too. She pulled a tissue out of her computer bag to dab her eyes.

I made myself laugh. "Why? Because we're buying sports bras?"

"Don't make fun, Lia. It's just the whole thing." Her voice was quivery. "Your mom taking me bra shopping when I was in seventh grade, now me taking you. It's like one big circle, you know?"

"I guess."

I thought she was going to launch into a speech about the circle of life, or maybe positive energy in the universe. But instead she said something that made my throat ache: "I wish Jessie could be doing this for you, buttercup. It's so unfair that she isn't. I know she would be so proud of how you're growing up, and I don't just mean in the boob department." Aunt Shelby kissed my forehead. "But if anyone besides Jessie has to be here with you right now, I'm very glad it's me."

We bought five un-weird sports bras that I could actually see myself wearing. In fact, as soon as we got home, I put one on.

I studied myself in the upstairs bathroom mirror. Did

I look any different? Not really. But that wasn't the point of these girl protectors, anyway.

"Lia?" Aunt Shelby was knocking on the bathroom door. "Do you by chance have any cocoa powder in this house? I'm preparing for this evening's festivities."

"Try the pantry above the fridge."

"Okay, thanks. And stay out of the kitchen!"

I didn't argue. But the word "cocoa" reminded me—I'd promised there'd be gobs of chocolate tonight. Dang.

I ran into my bedroom and took some money from my bank. As I was about to leave for the corner grocery store, Nate grabbed my elbow and pulled me into his room.

"What's going on, Lia?" he demanded.

I yanked my arm away. "What do you mean?"

"Everything. What Aunt Shelby's doing here again, why she's taking over the kitchen, what she means by 'festivities.'"

I didn't answer.

"I thought you were mad at her," he said.

"Yeah, I guess I was."

"But not now?"

I shrugged. "I still think she's crazy."

"So why are you going along with her craziness?"

I knew I couldn't explain it to him. After that morning in the mall, something had changed for me. It wasn't about the bra—or maybe it was, in a way. Because for the first time I felt a connection with my aunt that included my mom. And I knew that whatever crazy thing Aunt Shelby was concocting for me in the kitchen, it was as if my mom were cheering us on.

Chocolate Cake

I BOUGHT HERSHEY'S KISSES, TOOTSIE ROLLS, Kit Kat bars, and Snickers. Then I remembered Mak's obsession with Twizzlers, so I bought her a pack. Was that enough candy? Probably not. At the register I added a Milky Way, two Oh Henrys, and an Almond Joy. Also a couple of Dove Bars, a 3 Musketeers, and some tropical mix jelly beans.

By the time I got home it was a little after four. I still wasn't allowed in the kitchen, so I dumped the candy on the living room coffee table. It occurred to me that

I should get ready for the party-ish thing, but I had no idea how to dress. So I decided it was a come-as-you-are-party-ish-thing, and I'd just wear what I already had on—green sweater, jeans, new bra.

At five forty-five, Dad and Nate left the house together to get some sushi and maybe see this new robots-take-over-the-world movie that both of them kept talking about. At six ten the doorbell rang.

It was Mak. As soon as I opened the door, she put her hand over her mouth. "So, is Abi coming?" she murmured.

"I think. She didn't tell you?"

"I didn't ask."

That was strange, I thought. Maybe they were still fighting.

The second guest to arrive was Marley, wearing a Chicago Bears jersey a size too big for Nate.

"It's just us?" she asked hopefully, spotting Mak sitting on the sofa, still wearing her denim jacket, her shoulders hunched.

But the doorbell rang again almost immediately. There was Jules, smiling her Jules smile. Two steps behind her was Abi, her eyes narrowed and her arms folded across her chest.

Fun and games, I thought. *Woo.*

I knocked on the kitchen wall three times, the signal

for Aunt Shelby to join us. She came out of the kitchen looking like a witch's little sister, wearing a long, swingy purple dress, her hair in skinny braids, and carrying two lit candles. She put the candles on the coffee table and flicked off the living room lights.

"Welcome," she said, smiling a smile I didn't recognize.

Abi ignored her. "So what are we celebrating, anyway?"

"It's my twelve-and-five-twelfths birthday," I told her.

"Which obviously calls for cake," Aunt Shelby declared. We watched her go to the kitchen and return seconds later carrying a tall, slightly tilted layer cake smothered in dark chocolate frosting. On top she'd written AMALIA JESSICA in swirly yellow icing. But I guess she hadn't planned her spacing, so my name came out on three separate lines:

AMAL

IAJES

SICA

Aunt Shelby smiled as she put the cake on the coffee table. "I heard you girls liked chocolate cake, and this is my special recipe. I worked on it all day, so if you don't eat it, I'll be deeply offended."

She began cutting the cake into huge slices, which she passed around on paper plates she must have found in one of Mom's secret cabinets, the ones she'd used for storing holiday decorations. The plates had pictures of Santa's elves in ice skates, and I prayed none of my ex-friends would notice. Or the paper napkins, either, which were so pink and fairy princessy, they must have been left over from my six-year-old birthday party.

"Dig in," Aunt Shelby said, squeezing herself into the space on the sofa next to Mak. She balanced a skating-elf plate on her lap as she ate a huge, gooey bite of cake.

I took a forkful. It was chocolaty, all right—chocolate cake with chocolate filling between the layers, plus the chocolate frosting on top. But there was another flavor I couldn't identify. Cinnamon? No, not cinnamon. The extra flavor wasn't bad-tasting, just spicy and sharp. Probably one of my aunt's warped mystery ingredients. Could anyone else taste it? If they did, they were too polite to say anything.

I glanced at Aunt Shelby. Why were her eyes sparkling?

When Jules put down her fork, my aunt protested, "No, no, eat up." And as soon as Abi finished her slice, Aunt Shelby gave her another, which she insisted Abi finish completely.

At last the cake was almost gone.

"Now," Aunt Shelby said. "We're going to play a little party game I think you'll all recognize. It's based on Truth or Dare."

Mak groaned. "I am *so sick* of that game. Do we have to?"

"Oh, but this is a different version. In this version, there are only truths."

Abi snorted. "Yeah, well, some of us have a little problem with truths."

"Not this time," Aunt Shelby said.

"Why not?" I demanded, suddenly nervous.

"Because this cake contains a special ingredient from my herb store in Maine. It's called capsicum annuum, and it was used frequently by the ancient Aztecs."

"What for?" Marley asked.

"Truth-telling," Aunt Shelby said, nodding. "The Aztecs didn't have a justice system like we do, so when someone was accused of a crime, the local chiefs would give them capsicum annuum in powdered form. Then they'd ask the defendant questions."

Jules's eyes popped. "You mean it's like a *truth serum*?"

Aunt Shelby laughed. "Oh, there's no such thing. But the Aztecs believed this powder released certain toxins from the body, certain negative energies that resulted in hurtful speech and falsehoods. Can you already feel a bit warm? Those are the toxins rising to the surface of your skin. Doesn't it feel good to rid your bodies of all that negativity?"

I stared at my aunt. *She can't be serious*, I thought. *This is obviously one of her pretend potions!* But here was the strange thing: Even as I had this thought, I realized that my cheeks were burning.

Which was crazy, I told myself. Because Aunt Shelby was a total fake. She didn't have a clue what she was doing; she'd probably read about ancient Aztecs on Wikipedia.

Still, there was no question that right then my heart was pounding. My head felt light. And I realized I wanted to talk. I *needed* to talk.

It just felt like *my turn*, and I didn't even need someone to ask me a question.

"Can I go first?" I begged.

"You?" Aunt Shelby's eyebrows shot up; she looked a bit rattled. "Oh, okay, Lia, why not. Did you want me to ask you a—"

"I never got my period!" I interrupted. "I made it all up! The walk on the beach, the drips on my leg, the towel, the hoodie, everything."

"*Yesss!*" Marley shouted, punching the air with her fist. For a second I thought she'd do a spazzy victory dance, but she just sat on the sofa, grinning.

Abi smirked at me. "Yeah, Lia. I had a feeling."

"Really?" I tried to catch my breath. "Anything *you* want to share?"

"Me?"

"Your turn, Abi," I said. "Go ahead."

Everyone stared at her.

"Abi, why are you blushing?" Mak asked as she took off her jacket.

"It's the heat of the toxins, dear," Aunt Shelby told Abi. "No point resisting; the truth always prevails."

Abi started shredding her napkin into a small pile of pink confetti. "Fine, so I didn't get mine either, all right? I got cramps really bad the second week of camp, so I thought it was happening, but it never did, and I didn't want to tell anyone, because after the fuss I made—"

"So you lied about getting your period? Oh, wow." Mak gaped at her. "But why? Because you were jealous I'd gotten mine?"

Abi's eyes filled with tears. Her voice shook. "Don't be so judgy, Makayla. You have no idea—none—about how I feel all the time. Nothing is hard for you, ever! You do everything perfectly—"

"That's so not true!"

"You're beautiful, you're smart, you're this amazing musician, you win all these swimming competitions, everyone likes you—"

"They'd like *you* if you weren't so nasty."

"No, they wouldn't! I know your other friends all hate me!"

Mak groaned. "See, this is why—" She shook her head.

"Why what?" Aunt Shelby asked, patting Mak's knee.

"Why I can't just hang out with my other friends! Abi gets so jealous, I have to lie and say we're having a swim practice or something."

"Wait!" Abi cried. "Stop! Mak, you've been *lying* about swim practice?"

"Sometimes. Yeah."

"That's horrible," Jules exclaimed.

"Yeah, well, it's better than dealing with Abi's tantrums." Mak straightened her shoulders and took a deep breath. "I need to say something, Abi, all right? Lately you're either crying and yelling because I'm just talking to somebody else, or accusing me of stealing a boyfriend who wasn't even your boyfriend, or just acting nasty for no reason. You know, I really hated how you laughed when I hit Lia with the volleyball."

"And I didn't like that you wrote 'Liar' on her locker," Jules blurted.

Abi flinched as if she'd been slapped. "I just wrote 'Lia R.' I *told* you guys—"

"But we didn't believe it, Abi," Jules said softly. "Sorry."

"Don't *apologize* to her," Mak snapped.

"Sorry."

"Don't apologize to *me*, Jules."

Nobody spoke. It was like everyone was in shock.

All of a sudden Abi turned to me. Her eyes were blazing.

"Okay, since we all ate the cake, Lia, why don't you tell us the truth about Tanner?"

Aunt Shelby blinked at me. "Oh, Lia, they know about Tanner?"

She'd forgotten? But I'd told her about my Tanner story when we were on the phone. I was sure of it.

"Um. Yes?" I said.

"Well, I'm gobsmacked," Aunt Shelby said. "I didn't know Tanner was a topic you even discussed."

Abi snorted. "You mean he exists?"

"Oh, he exists, all right," Aunt Shelby said. "But I'm afraid aunts don't give details about nieces and their first kisses, even with capsicum annuum, because there are some bonds that are sacred, so to speak, and when a lovely, gorgeous boy's heart is broken, well . . . Ask me anything else. We simply won't discuss Tanner."

I stared at my aunt. Why was she lying about Tanner? The whole point of this party was to tell the truth. To rid negativity, or toxins, or—

"That's so unfair!" Abi protested to Aunt Shelby. "You can't just refuse to answer a question! Not if *we* can't!" She looked at Jules like she was expecting Jules to stick up for her.

But Jules stood. "This is too weird. I'm leaving, you guys."

"So am I," Marley said.

Abi pointed an accusing finger at her. "Yeah, Marley. You're always running off, right? What's the truth *you've* been hiding all this time?"

Aunt Shelby gave Marley a questioning look.

"I'd rather not talk about it now," Marley answered. "But actually, there's something I *do* want to say." She faced my aunt. "I think you were wrong to Aztec-herb us without our permission."

"I completely agree," I said.

"Ha," Abi snarled. "You probably knew all along, Lia. You probably helped your aunt bake that cake!"

"I did not!"

"Yeah, Lia, we totally believe you. Because you're so good at the truth, right?"

Up until then Marley had been almost silent and, except for celebrating my confession, almost calm. But when Abi said that to me, Marley exploded. "Shut up, Abi! You lied too—so you have no reason to pick on Lia. Or anybody else, for that matter. And you know what? I'm sick of how mean and moody you always are. *Everybody* is."

Abi's face went white. I'd never seen any resemblance before, but in that instant she looked exactly like Val that time in my kitchen when I'd reminded her of the way she'd bullied my aunt in middle school.

Aunt Shelby must have seen Abi's reaction too; maybe that was why she picked that moment to speak up. "Time-out, girls," she announced. She reached into a dress pocket and pulled out a small plastic sandwich bag filled with a red powder. "Behold my secret ingredient, the ancient Aztec herb capsicum annuum! Otherwise known as cayenne pepper."

"That's what you put in the *cake?*" I stared at my aunt. "Regular old cayenne pepper?"

"Just a pinch, buttercup. No harm, no worries. Actually, I thought it tasted kind of good with all that chocolate."

"But why?" I could barely form words. "Why did you do that?"

"Ah. So here's the punchline of my little joke: *game over.* No more Truth or Dare, or any version of it, either. Because real friends treat each other as equals. They don't force things on each other. Or *from* each other."

"But *you* forced that cake on *us*," Abi protested. "And then you forced us to say things!"

"Actually, dear, everyone spoke on their own," Aunt Shelby replied. She waved her arm as if she held an invisible fairy wand. "And now that you've expressed your truths to each other, no one has more power than anyone else, balance has been restored, and you can all move forward in a positive direction. No more negativity, all right? There are already too many dark clouds in this world, and we're all better off living in sunshine. Can we agree on that, girls?"

My ex-friends gaped as Aunt Shelby twirled to take the almost-empty cake plate back into the kitchen.

I didn't know whether to laugh or cry.

"Omigod," I sputtered. "You guys, I am so, so sorry. But I bought tons of chocolate, like I promised. And other stuff too. So please help yourselves—" I gestured wildly toward the candy still piled up on the coffee table.

Abi flew out the door, with Jules following. Mak nodded at me and mumbled, "See you, Lia," as she grabbed her jacket and walked out.

That left Marley.

"Marley, I don't know what to say—" I began.

She took a Milky Way and also shoved a Snickers bar into her pants pocket. "Well, anyhow, you were right about one thing. This definitely wasn't a boring pizza-and-bowling party."

Agate

IN THE KITCHEN, AUNT SHELBY WAS CALMLY drinking a glass of orange juice. As soon as she saw me, she did a little jig that sloshed some juice on the floor.

"Wasn't that brilliant?" she demanded, laughing. "Didn't you love it—'Aztec truth powder'?"

"It *was* kind of clever," I admitted. "But it didn't solve anything."

She put down the glass. "What do you mean?"

I sighed. "I thought this was going to be a *party*. And at

the end of it, we would all magically be friends again. But now everyone's upset. At *me*."

"Why at you?"

"Because you're my aunt. And you basically just had us ambush Abi."

"Who was bullying *all* your friends, Lia. Not just you."

"How can you say that? You don't even know them!"

"No, but Val does."

"What?"

"Val's told me stuff. She's been paying close attention."

"But—I don't understand," I sputtered. "She told you her own *daughter* was a bully?"

My aunt nodded. "Val's been worried about it for a while. She tried talking to Abi, but Abi wouldn't listen. And when you reminded her of her own behavior in middle school toward *me*—"

"Aunt Shelby, that was a totally different situation!"

"—it made her wonder if bullying was genetic. Or if somehow she was enabling Abi's behavior. So she talked to me about it."

"Why to *you*?"

"Lia, I know you don't think I know anything about herbs—"

"I never said you didn't know *anything*."

"—but I do know a middle school bully when I see one. And I do know a victim. All you girls were kissing a bully's bahooties, and now you won't have to."

"Bahooties?" I repeated. "What's that?"

She grinned. "Nothing. I just made it up. But you get the point, right?"

It all seemed so simple to my aunt, like prescribing someone a "treatment." Or handing someone a crystal. *Put it under your pillow. And poof: no more insomnia.* Or, *Here's a leaf. Poof: Now you're pregnant.*

"What's wrong?" She frowned at me.

"Aunt Shelby," I said, "I know you had a hard time in middle school and you never got over it. And I know you thought you were helping me with that cake. But now we've all said terrble stuff to each other that we can't take back!"

"Yes, but why would you *want* to?"

"To be friends again," I wailed.

Aunt Shelby shook her braids. "All right, Lia, you've lost me. Didn't you tell me you weren't sure you *wanted* to be friends with these girls?"

"Yeah. But maybe I changed my mind. Anyway, it was before *this*."

As I said these words, I felt like a party piñata that had been smashed open. I was deflated, empty. Without my friends, who could I talk to? I had no one now—no mom, a dad I loved but who couldn't really understand, a brother who teased, a crazy aunt. Bad friends were better than no friends, right?

Aunt Shelby rushed over to give me a hug that basically kept me upright. "Lia," she said in my ear. "I know these girls were there for you in the past, especially when your mom died. But you're all growing and changing, and if these friendships aren't working out for you anymore, you shouldn't be afraid to let them go. Believe me, sweetheart, I know your mom wanted you to have *true* friends, girls who support each other, who have each other's back. Someone like Marley—"

I pulled away. "You told me you fought with Mom all the time! How can you say you know what she wanted?"

"Because she was my sister," Aunt Shelby said quietly. "And you know what, buttercup? She still is."

That night I slept a million hours. It was as if I'd never slept before and couldn't figure out how to stop.

When I finally woke, I spent a long time staring at the ceiling. Yesterday had been truly horrific, the way Aunt Shelby had organized a party so that we could all attack Abi. And even if Abi had deserved it, even if she was the cause of all the fighting, my mom—the Jessie who'd figured out how to stop Shelby's bullies—would never have humiliated one of my friends. So if Aunt Shelby "knew" what my mom would've wanted, why had she allowed a thing like that to happen?

Then I thought about Mak finally speaking her mind and how even Jules had stood up to Abi for the first time in history. So maybe the party hadn't been such a disaster after all, I told myself. Aunt Shelby had tricked us with that cake—but really, my ex-friends hadn't needed much of an excuse to tell off Abi.

And I was glad I'd told the truth about my period. Finally. I still owed the truth about kissing Tanner, even though everyone had probably figured it out by now anyway. Although it was strange that Aunt Shelby had covered up for me. Considering how she was all for truth and sunshine, blah, blah, blah, lying about Tanner didn't make much sense.

Then I had this crazy thought: *Maybe she lied about Tanner because she cares about me. And maybe she thought it was what I wanted.*

That was when I noticed an envelope on the floor, which must have been slipped under my door while I was sleeping. I got out of bed to open it.

Inside was a small blue stone and a note from my aunt.

Dear Lia,

Sorry I messed up. Your mom was so much better at mom stuff—and I know I'm not much of a substitute. But I was only trying to protect you. That's something I'll never stop doing. Anyway, I doubt there will be any more trouble.

xoxox,

Aunt S

PS. Here's an agate. Keep it by your bedside. The ancient Aztecs used it to ward off bullies and meanies.

PPS. Late bloomers unite!

PPPS. Marley seems like a good friend. Just my intuition.

PPPPS. Tanner is a nice boy, but he's not very bright. For a first kiss, pick someone better, okay? 😊

PPPPPS. Talk to you soon!

Apologies

AFTER I GOT DRESSED, I RAN OVER TO ABI'S HOUSE. When I rang the doorbell, Val answered.

"Can I please speak to Abi?" I asked.

"Sorry, Lia," Val said quietly. "She's not here right now."

I thought it was a lie, that Abi was simply too hurt and angry to see me. But then Val added: "She and Jules went to the movies. But I'm meeting her for dinner at the diner. You're welcome to join us."

Really? This was an invitation. So it meant Val had forgiven me for calling her a bully?

"That would be great," I said eagerly. "What time?"

"Six," she said.

I went home, did some homework, washed my hair. At five thirty I told Dad I was having dinner with Val and Abi. He looked startled, which made me wonder if Aunt Shelby had told him about the party. But he didn't ask questions or say I couldn't go; in fact, he drove me to the diner.

Val and Abi were at the same table I'd shared with Graydon. When was that? Only a few days ago, but it felt like weeks.

I could tell Val hadn't told Abi she'd invited me, because as soon as I walked over, Abi's face paled. She put down her fork.

"Lia, what are you doing here?" she asked in a flat voice.

"I came to talk to you. It'll be fast."

"You know what? While you girls are chatting, I think I'll take a potty break," Val announced. Under other circumstances, Abi and I would have giggled at "potty break," but Abi just glared as I slid into Val's seat.

"So what is it?" she said, almost spitting out the words.

"I want to apologize," I said.

"Yeah? For what?"

"The party. I thought it was going to be the opposite of how it was. I had no idea that my aunt would make everyone hurt you."

Abi raised one eyebrow. "That's exactly what she did, you know. I felt attacked."

"I know. We talked about it afterward, and I told her so. The thing is, my aunt has this thing about bullying, because she was bullied in middle school. And she just wants to make sure I'm okay."

I could see Abi was interested. I could also see that she hadn't heard anything about Aunt Shelby's bullying before. So if I wanted to, I could have told Abi right then that her own mom was the bully—sweet, generous, cupcake-baking Val.

But I couldn't.

If she was going to find out that Val stuffed undershirts in my aunt's gym locker and called her names, it would be Val who told her, not me. I wasn't going to take Abi's perfect mom from her. After everything that had happened, I felt like I owed that much to Abi. Even more, I owed that to Val. And in a strange way I couldn't explain, I also felt that I owed it to my mom.

"Anyway," I said, "I came to tell you I'm sorry about what happened at my house. Although I do agree with my aunt about one thing. The way we played that Truth or Dare game was really nasty. But I forgive you, Abi."

"*You* forgive *me?* Oh, that's hilarious, Lia."

"I also forgive you for lying about your period."

I can't say exactly when Val had returned from her potty break, but it was right then that I realized she was standing behind me.

"What?" She looked horrified. "Abi, you lied to your friends about—?"

Oh no, I thought. It was like I couldn't stop getting Abi in trouble. *Maybe I should just get out of here.*

"Sorry for interrupting your dinner," I murmured as I slipped out of the seat.

Of course I realized that Abi and I would never be best friends again. And of course I realized the same would go for Jules. Because that's just the way it was with those two.

Mak was different. On Monday I showed up at school with the pack of Twizzlers I'd bought for the party. I put it on her desk in homeroom.

"They're apology Twizzlers," I explained.

"You mean for that crazy party?" she asked, rolling her eyes. "But it wasn't your fault, Lia. And anyway, the whole thing was for the best."

"It was?"

"Abi needed to hear all that. We should have said that stuff a long time ago. And I'm sorry I went along with any of it."

"You did? I don't even remember, Mak."

"Makayla," she corrected me, smiling a little bashfully. "And thanks, Lia. But yeah, I totally did."

She ripped open the pack of Twizzlers with her teeth. We weren't supposed to eat in homeroom, it was just after breakfast, and the truth was, I didn't especially like Twizzlers. But when she handed me the pack, I took one to be polite.

Makayla looked blissed out as she chomped on the fake-red candy stick. "My long-lost love," she said in a swoony voice, sighing like a heroine in a bad romance movie.

Superpowers

THE THING ABOUT LOSING YOUR FRIENDS: YOU gain superpowers. Two in particular—Invisibility, which means you can go anywhere without people noticing, and Super Vision, which means you see things in sharper focus than you ever have before.

So even though, for example, you have nowhere to sit at lunch, you can plop yourself at any table and no one will mind. (Because basically, they don't see you.) And from your perch, wherever you seat yourself, you get to observe things. The sort of things that were always there but that you just never noticed.

For example: the fact that Abi and Jules were in their own little friend bubble. At lunch they barely talked to anybody else in the entire grade, male or female. How was it possible that I'd never even picked up on this before? I watched them sit huddled together in the lunchroom for a whole week before I saw Jules chat with another human being (Cooper Chang, who had dimples and ridiculously long eyelashes). Afterward, Abi looked upset, like she was scolding Jules for ignoring her. And Jules said some things back, like she was sticking up for herself, finally. The next day, and the day after that, I saw Jules laughing with Cooper at the salad bar. *Go, Jules*, I chanted in my brain. Maybe the friend bubble had popped a little. I hoped so.

I also noticed Makayla dividing her lunchtime between her swim friends and her band friends. Often she started with one group and ended with another; sometimes the groups overlapped and she switched seats anyway. I think she was relieved to not have to hide her social life from Abi anymore. And honestly, I was glad for her.

But I didn't sit with her. It may seem funny to say this after all the time we spent together, but I realized that Makayla and I were never actually friends. It was more like we were both in the same family—a family headed by Abi. And when the family fell apart, Makayla drifted away. We still chatted together in homeroom, and I was grateful for the nice things she'd said after the party, but we'd never hang out again outside school. This made me sad to think—but with my new Super Vision, I could see how relaxed her shoulders looked now, how loudly she laughed, how she belonged with her other friends. And here's another funny thing I realized: We didn't have a whole lot in common, anyway.

As for Marley: In homeroom she sketched all the time, making it seem that she didn't want to talk to anybody, including (or maybe especially) me. I never saw her in the lunchroom, which made me assume she was with Graydon in the computer lab. She didn't invite me to join them, but I wondered if I should barge in anyway. Although I'd be sitting there eating my yogurt while they played a game I knew nothing about and would probably stink at if I tried to play.

Plus, there was the whole Graydon thing. Makayla had said that he still liked me, but it was hard to believe, and after the diner fiasco, I didn't want to take any chances. What if I asked if I could join him for lunch and he said no? I cringed just imagining that whole scene. Plus, the thing about Invisibility: It stops working when you're in a small group. Squeezing my way into the Marley-Graydon-Ben-Jake circle would mean surrendering my superpowers.

Which was possibly the right thing to do. But for what felt like a long time after the party, I ate lunch with nobody, or else with Ruby Lewis (who was now wearing a bra every day, thanks to Mrs. Garcia). And my superpowers stayed intact.

By then a couple of weeks had gone by with no dinners from Val. If Dad was surprised about this, he didn't mention it. The truth was, it was kind of a nice feeling that we Rollinses could manage dinner on our own.

But on the last Tuesday in September, Val showed up with two shopping bags full of food. I knew she'd forgiven me, and since she was friends now with Aunt Shelby, she must have decided she should start feeding us again.

Dad asked her into the kitchen, where he was roasting a chicken. He opened the oven to show it to her.

"That's beautiful!" she exclaimed. "And it smells delicious! Kevin, you've learned to cook?"

"From YouTube." He grinned. "Would you like to join us for dinner?"

"Oh, no, I have dinner waiting at home. But thanks!"

He took her hand then—not to shake it, but to hold it. "Val, you've been . . . I can't even begin to tell you how much we all appreciate everything you've done. But I think we can take it from here."

Val smiled, burst into tears, nodded, blew us all kisses, and ran out with the shopping bags—although fortunately, she left behind a tray of brownies.

A few days after that my aunt showed up in her truck.

"Look what Benchley Rescues rescued!" she shouted as she honked her horn in our driveway.

Nate and I peered in the window of the cab. In the passenger seat was a pet carrier—and inside were two calico cats, a big one and a tiny one, obviously a mom and her kitten.

"Did you drive them all the way here just to visit?" Nate wrinkled his nose as if they smelled bad. I could tell he'd inherited my mom's cat-hating gene.

"Nope," Aunt Shelby said. She grinned at me. "These are anti-birthday presents for Lia."

"Seriously?" I squeaked. "For me?"

"Don't worry. I asked your dad first and he completely agreed."

"I agreed to *one* cat," Dad said, coming out to the driveway.

"Yes, Kevin, technically you did," Aunt Shelby said. "But these cuties were too sweet to separate. And you know, we should honor the mother-daughter bond."

I had to laugh. Aunt Shelby had no shame—she'd say

anything to anybody. I thought Dad might be offended with her sneaky "mother-daughter" mention and the way he was being guilted into letting me keep both cats, but I could see that he was trying not to smile.

"Okay, Shel, you win. *If* Lia even wants them." He winked at me.

"Are you crazy?" I squealed. "Let me hold them!"

We took the carrier inside. Aunt Shelby said I should keep the cats in my room for now, so that they wouldn't get overwhelmed by a whole house. I didn't argue—if Aunt Shelby was an expert on any topic, it was cats.

When we were upstairs in my bedroom, with the door shut tight, she opened the carrier. First the mother cat poked out her head, sniffing the air suspiciously. Then out came the kitten, a miniature version of the mom, except for a black freckle on her pink nose, a peanut-shaped orange spot on her side, and a black mark on one ear that looked sort of like a tiny comma.

"Thank you, Aunt Shelby," I whispered.

As soon as I'd spoken those words, I realized I hadn't said them in a long time. Maybe ever.

My aunt hugged me. "They're actually a thank-*you* present. It's because of *you* that I patched things up with Val. And guess what—she's agreed to invest in my new store. Isn't that incredible?"

"It really is," I said. Although the thought of Aunt Shelby and Val working together was a bit *King Kong Meets Godzilla for Brunch*. Or no: *King Kong 'n' Godzilla: BFFs at Last*.

Aunt Shelby pulled out of the hug. "We're okay again, then, Lia? You and me?"

I nodded.

"So how are you, buttercup? Your friends still angry?"

I shook my head.

"And everything's good again?"

I shook my head.

"Cat got your tongue?"

"Haha." I sighed. "We're not enemies, but we're not really friends anymore. I guess the whole thing just got too weird."

Aunt Shelby picked up the kitten and handed her to me. "What about Marley?"

"What about her?"

"She's a good one, Lia. Don't give up so easily."

I didn't reply. I buried my face in the kitten's fuzzy fur.

"Lia," my aunt said quietly, "I need to say something important, so please listen: You aren't just some boring 'nice' girl; you're a *fighter*. You've proven that to me over and over. So fight for your friendship! Be fierce! You still have that agate I gave you?"

"Yeah." It was in a box under my bed, waiting for other crystals.

"Wear it to school on Monday; it'll give you strength."

"Aunt Shelby—"

"Don't 'Aunt Shelby' me, niecelet. Or I'll ground you." She laughed. "Did I say that right? Like a mom?"

"Yeah," I said, grinning.

She nearly shoved me off my bed. "Hey, look at me, getting the hang of this thing."

Firsts

OVER THE WEEKEND I'D DECIDED TO NAME THE mother cat Amethyst and the kitten Agate as a way of thanking Aunt Shelby, who was so happy when I told her that she burst into tears.

"But for short I'm calling them Amy and Aggie," I informed her as she dabbed her eyes with a tissue. I mean, I wanted to thank my aunt, but I didn't want her to think I'd gone all crystal crazy in gratitude.

Also, I starting thinking that Aunt Shelby would drive me nuts asking for constant updates on the cats. So I decided it was time to ask Dad for a cell phone again. At least that way I could send her photos. And anyway, it was probably time.

On Monday I stuffed the blue agate into my jeans pocket. At lunch I squeezed it as I walked into the computer lab.

Marley pushed her bangs out of her eyes as she looked up at me. "Hey," she said. "So you finally came back. We were wondering if you'd ever show."

I blinked. "Really? Why didn't you just invite me, then?"

"You were waiting for an invitation? Like in a seashell or something?" She snorted. "Oh, whatever. Pull up a chair."

I did. Every day at lunch. Pretty soon I got decent at Phantom. Decent enough to do a victory dance a couple of times, although I was nowhere near as obnoxious about it as Marley.

The weeks passed. Nothing changed very much, except that I lost my superpowers.

Oh, but this happened: I had my first kiss. On Halloween, Marley, Ruby, Graydon, Ben, Jake, and I went ironic trick-or-treating. We didn't wear costumes like little kids, but we all spray-painted our hair crazy colors and wore our clothes backward. When our bags were full and we'd eaten ridiculous amounts of candy, Marley invited us over to watch a scary movie.

Just as we got to her front door, Graydon poked me on the shoulder. "Can we talk a second?" he said.

"Sure," I replied. "What's up?"

"Remember that thing you asked me?"

I stared at his green hair, how it clashed with his orange eyebrows. "No. What thing?"

"In the diner that time."

"Oh. Right."

"You still—?" He looked at his sneakers, which were on the wrong feet.

"Sure," I said quickly, my heart banging.

We waited for everyone to go inside. He climbed a step so he could be as tall as me. Then he leaned toward me and we kissed.

His lips tasted like Snickers. Mine probably tasted like 3 Musketeers.

The whole thing lasted maybe three seconds. And we both pulled away at exactly the same time, then stood there, grinning at each other.

"Well, that was unprecedented," he said.

And also this: A few Friday afternoons after that, Marley and I were in the diner with practically the entire seventh grade. We were sipping our milk shakes, talking about the HiberNation trilogy, when my phone rang. By then I'd gotten used to the fact that I had a phone again and that Dad and Aunt Shelby were calling me all the time. But when I realized the caller was Val, I was kind of shocked. I mean, I hadn't seen or heard from her in a couple of months. I didn't even know how she had my number.

She said she was calling to invite me over for dinner. That very night.

My first reaction was, *Yay! Val's cooking!*

My second reaction: *Oh, but Abi.*

We weren't enemies. But we weren't friends. Maybe things would change sometime in the future, but right now we said hi when we passed in the hall and that was it. So the thought of sitting in Abi's kitchen, listening to her tell her mom about her day at school—

"Oh, that's really nice of you," I told Val. "I'd love to come. Although could we please make it some other time? I'm not feeling so great today."

"You're not?" I could hear her shift into concerned-mom mode. "What's wrong, Lia? What are your symptoms? Do you have a fever?"

"No, no. I just, you know, have my period and I'm really tired, so I think I'll hang out at home tonight. But thanks!"

Across the table, Marley slurped her milk shake loudly.

As soon as I hung up with Val, Marley said, "Hmm. Still lying about the period thing, I see."

"It was just a little fib," I insisted. "A white lie."

"Dude, I'm teasing. Chill, okay?"

Still, I felt weird after that call. Even just thinking about Val and Abi and all the real lying I'd done this year made my stomach hurt. In fact, it started to hurt so much I couldn't even finish my milk shake. Finally I got up to use the bathroom.

And guess what.

Wait, really? I thought. I hadn't had any symptoms; I was totally unprepared. A million times I'd imagined how it would happen (if it ever did)—and in every version I came up with, it was always at school, where Mrs. Garcia would say comforting things and give me a Tylenol and a pad and let me hang out on her cot for the rest of the day. And maybe call Dad to say something like, *Lia is a bit under the weather, nothing serious, but it's* that time, *so please treat her with special understanding. Oh, and I'd advise unlimited chocolate.*

I'd never even considered it could happen anywhere else, under any other circumstances. Probably this was payback for lying to Val.

I speed-dialed Aunt Shelby.

"Niecelet! Welcome to womanhood!" Her voice sounded all teary and wobbly.

"But what do I *do?* I'm stuck at the diner. It's Friday afternoon, so the entire *school* is here. I can't just walk out there like this!"

"Like what? Lia, it's not showing, is it?"

"No, but I'm wearing a *skirt.* What if something happens?"

I thought about fake Tanner, how he'd loaned me his towel. That was so nice of him, in a fake sort of way. Of course, in real life, your first period happened in a diner bathroom, not on a romantic beach.

"Aunt Shelby?" I squeaked. "Are you *there*?"

"Lia, don't panic."

And I bet now she'll just tell me to squeeze an amethyst or something, I thought.

But she surprised me.

"Is Marley there with you?" she asked.

"Yeah, back at our table. Why?"

"Text her. Tell her to come."

"What for?"

"Just do it, buttercup. And call me tonight! I want to hear everything!"

So I texted Marley: *Pls meet me in bathrm.*

She burst in immediately, wearing her backpack. "You okay? I need to leave for tutoring."

I told her what happened. She unzipped her backpack, handed me a pad, then took off her Chicago Cubs hoodie.

"Put this on," she said. "It's so big it'll cover you. No one will notice anything."

"Thanks." I put on her hoodie, which practically reached my knees. Perfect! Lucky for me that Marley wore crazy-big clothes and that she just happened to have pads in her backpack!

Then it hit me: *Marley had pads in her backpack.*

"Marley, why do you have . . . ?" I started. "I mean, does this mean . . . ? So you get your period?"

She nodded.

"Since when?"

"Last summer in Chicago."

"You got your period *last summer*? You've had it this *entire year*?"

Marley shrugged. "Yeah."

"And my aunt figured it out? That's why she told me to text you just now?"

"I guess."

"How did she know?"

"No clue. I didn't tell her."

"But you never—" I sputtered. "How come you didn't tell *me*?"

"Because we're friends. Right?"

I nodded. Yes, Marley and I were definitely friends. Best friends, in fact.

"And I didn't want you to feel left behind," she said simply. "Now let's get out of here, okay?"

"But what if—"

"Lia, I promise it'll be fine. I'll walk in back of you. Just go!"

So we left the diner together, me in front and my best friend right behind me.

Acknowledgments

This book is a bit different for me, so I'm especially grateful to my wonderful editor, Alyson Heller, for allowing me to spread my wings.

Once again, deepest thanks to my agent, Jill Grinberg, for nurturing this book from conception to birth. Thanks to the whole expert team at Jill Grinberg Literary Management: Katelyn Detweiler, Cheryl Pientka, and Denise St. Pierre.

Thanks to all the inspired folks at Aladdin/Simon & Schuster, including Fiona Simpson, Laura Lyn DiSiena, Jeanine Henderson, and Mandy Veloso. Special thanks to Mara Anastas for starting the conversation, and supporting this project all the way through!

Lizzy, Jamie, Tom, Aaron, and Morgan: thanks for the cat names!

Big hugs to Lizzy, Josh, Alex, and Dani. Lizzy, your feedback was infinitely helpful, as always. Mom, thanks for encouraging. And Chris, thanks for being my first reader, true love, and best friend.

About the Author

Barbara Dee is the author of *The (Almost) Perfect Guide to Imperfect Boys*, *Trauma Queen*, *This Is Me From Now On*, *Solving Zoe* (Bank Street Best Children's Books) and *Just Another Day in My Insanely Real Life* (Publishers Weekly starred review). Her next book, *Star-Crossed*, will be published by Aladdin/Simon & Schuster in spring 2017. Barbara is one of the founders and directors of the Chappaqua Children's Book Festival. She lives in Westchester County, New York, with her family, two naughty cats, and a rescue hound dog named Ripley. Barbara blogs at Fromthemixedupfiles.com. Read more about Barbara at BarbaraDeeBooks.com.